D1491299

Based on the TV series *Rugrats*® created by Arlene Klasky, Gabor Csupo, and Paul Germain, and *The Wild Thornberrys*® created by Klasky Csupo Inc., as seen on Nickelodeon®.

SIMON SPOTLIGHT
An imprint of Simon & Schuster Children's Publishing Division
1230 Avenue of the Americas, New York, New York 10020

Bathysphere spot art on pages six and seven of the insert, and boat deck scene and Nigel and Marianne spot on page eight of the insert illustrated by Patrick Dene, Bradley J. Gake, and Mike Giles.

Manufactured in the United States of America
First Edition
2 4 6 8 10 9 7 5 3

ISBN 0-689-85431-5

Library of Congress Control Number 2002113620

by Cathy East Dubowski
based on the screenplay written
by Kate Boutilier

Simon Spotlight/Nickelodeon
New York   London   Toronto   Sydney   Singapore

CHAPTER

Tommy Pickles was in paradise. Before him were lush green forests, thundering waterfalls, mountain peaks, and the winding Amazon River. Exotic birds chirped in the trees, colorful frogs hopped through the leaves, and monkeys swung through the branches.

Tommy, with his bushy red mustache, spoke into a camera that filmed his every move.

"Come along, faithful viewers, on our journey through the drain forest, as we search for that rare and unusable creature—the three-toed sloth!"

Tommy pushed aside the thick brush, and his eyes lit up at what he saw: a sleeping sloth, clutching a banana in its paws. "Ah, there he is—teething with life!" Tommy said in a loud whisper. He began to tiptoe toward the strange-looking animal. "Let's get a closer look, shall we?"

"Closer?" exclaimed Chuckie Finster—Tommy's best friend and backyard-famous documentary film director. "Oh, no, you don't." He raised his megaphone and shouted, "Cut! Cut!"

Tommy's friends had gathered to watch. Twin playmates Phil and Lil were operating the camera. Kimi, Chuckie's younger sister, waited in a nearby Jeep.

"Don't worry, Chuckie," Tommy assured him. "I'm Nigel Strawberry, wild aminal eggspert—"

Suddenly a tiger sprang from the bushes and roared, baring its sharp teeth.

"And 'cause I'm an eggspert," Tommy continued, "I say—everybody, into the truck!"

The young nature crew ran toward their Jeep. Chuckie leaped into a seat next to Kimi. Phil and Lil quickly piled into the backseat.

Chuckie reached over and slammed the gas pedal.

The Jeep roared off as Tommy raced behind them with the ferocious tiger at his heels.

Lil pointed the camera at him. "Say something, Nigel."

Tommy gasped for breath as he ran. "Uh, uh, I can hear the tiger's running feets . . ." —he glanced over his shoulder—"and see his sharp teeth—"

The tiger snapped at Tommy's behind. Its sharp teeth snagged his pants and pulled them down.

"—and, um, feel a cool breeze!" Tommy concluded. He yanked up his pants just as Phil pulled him into the backseat of the Jeep. The Jeep hit a bump, flew into the air . . .

And landed with a *splash!* in the murky river.

The Jeep wouldn't budge. It was stuck! Then the motor shut off. Kimi gulped. "Uh-oh." Frantically she tried to restart the Jeep.

A huge scary shape slithered toward them.

"Crockydile!" Kimi shouted.

"Crockagator!" Chuckie screamed. "Look out!" He climbed into the backseat, struggling to get away. Then he clutched Tommy's safari shirt. "What do we do now, Tommy? I mean, Nigel?"

The fearsome crocodile stopped to scratch the side of his head with his back leg.

"Not to worry, guys!" Tommy shouted fearlessly. He reached into his pocket, searching for something with which to fight off the croc, and pulled out a dog chew toy.

Tommy reared back and threw it with all his might. It bounced off the head of the crocodile—*squeak!*—then splashed into the water.

Instantly the crocodile dived for the toy.

Chuckie shook his sister's shoulder. "Okay, let's go now, Kimi, afore that crockagator comes back!"

Kimi tried again to start the engine. But it wouldn't go.

"Oh, no! Our truck's broked!"

Now even Tommy looked nervous. "But that was my onliest chew toy!"

"Then feed him Phil!" Chuckie shouted.

Phil scowled. "I heard that."

Tommy scrambled out of the Jeep and

began to slosh through the river. The water was waist high. His friends were right behind him. Lil held the camera up over her head.

In the distance Tommy spotted something. It looked like—a camp!

"That way!" he shouted, and he led them through the swamp.

But soon something strange began to happen. The babies began to sink!

"Whoa! What kind of mud is this?" Phil exclaimed.

"I'll ask the wild stuff eggspert," said Lil. She yanked on Tommy's sleeve. "Nigel, why are we sinking?"

"Quitsand!" Tommy cried out. "I shoulda knowed!"

"But you know what to do now . . . right?" Chuckie asked nervously.

Tommy looked around. Then he spotted a long thick vine!

Tommy lunged toward the hanging vine and grabbed on to the end. "Guys! Hang on to me!"

The babies trudged through the quicksand

till they reached their leader. Then Tommy pulled and pulled.

But it was no use. He couldn't pull them free. They were still stuck.

Suddenly the crocodile started to slink toward them.

Tommy and his friends screamed!

The crocodile's huge jaws yawned open. *SNAP!* Its teeth chomped down . . . on the end of the vine. Then the short crocodile walked off along the shore, dragging the babies out of the quicksand.

The babies cheered at their good fortune—until they heard a growl on the riverbank.

The babies screamed again.

A Siberian tiger stood on the edge of the quicksand, pawing the ground.

CHAPTER 2

Tommy blinked—and the Siberian Tiger turned into his bossy three-year-old cousin, Angelica.

Tommy sighed. Angelica had a way of making even the best imaginary adventures disappear. "You'd be screaming, too, Angelica, if you was chased by a Sifearean tiger and a crokagator—"

"Oh, brother," Angelica interrupted. "Were you pretending to be Nigel Strawberry again, Tommy?"

Tommy smiled. "Yeah! He's my hero. And when I grow up, I want to be just like him."

"Pickles, you're no Nigel Strawberry," Angelica snapped. "You're not even a Nigel

Raspberry!" She stuck out her tongue and made a raspberry sound. "You're just a back-yard baby with a diaper full of dreams."

Tommy's heart sank as he watched Angelica scoop up Fluffy and stomp off.

"Wow. She's mean," Phil said. But then he shrugged and turned back to his friends, ready for the next game. "Okay, who wants to go look for cookies under stuffs?"

The babies quickly raced into the house. All except Tommy.

Sighing, he tottered over to the patio. A barefoot Grandpa Lou, sprawled in a lawn chair, snored in front of a small television.

But when Tommy saw what show was on, he instantly cheered up. It was *Sir Nigel Thornberry's Animal World.* He toddled closer to see.

Nigel Thornberry's bright red hair and mus-tache flashed against the deep greens of the rain forest as a jaguar chased him through the jungle. As he ran he called over his shoulder to the shaky camera, "The *Panthera onca,* com-monly known as the jaguar, seems determined to feast on my nether regions." Nigel panted for breath, then flashed the audience a smile. "But not to worry . . ."

Nigel raced toward a river and leaped into a canoe drifting along the banks—just a few feet ahead of the jaguar's teeth.

Tommy sighed in relief.

But then, just as Nigel started to paddle away—

A crocodile sprang up from the murky water! It flipped the canoe.

Splash! Nigel disappeared beneath the water.

But seconds later he resurfaced and clung to the side of the overturned boat. Just in time he grabbed the canoe's paddle and jabbed at the crocodile.

"Well, faithful viewers, our journey was a smashing success!" Nigel announced, smiling broadly beneath his dripping mustache. "Until next time, this is Sir Nigel Thornberry of *Sir Nigel Thornberry's Animal World.*"

Grandpa Lou awoke with a start and squinted through his glasses at the TV as the show's theme music began to play. Then he noticed Tommy. "Why, hello, Scout. Boy, rest your eyes for a second, and ol' Thornberry's gator bait!"

Lou lifted his grandson into his lap. "Hey, boy, that Nigel gets in some real scrapes out there in the wild," he said. "But he always manages to wiggle out of trouble somehow."

C H A P T E R 3

The Pickleses' living room was a total mess. But for once it wasn't the babies' fault. Tommy and all his friends—and all his friends' mommies and daddies—were going on vacation.

Tommy's mother, Didi, staggered into the living room loaded down with toys that she added to an already huge pile. Phil and Lil's mom, Betty, wheeled several suitcases in through the front door. Their dad, Howard, dragged in some weights.

Angelica's mother, Charlotte, was talking into her cell phone. "Oh, and Jonathan," she told her assistant, "don't think that just because I'm on a luxury Lipschitz cruise in the

South China Sea, I won't be checking messages, e-mail, and carrier pigeons on the hour."

"Honey," said her husband, Drew, "I thought we were going to leave work behind for seven fun-filled days."

"Silly, it's not all work," Charlotte replied. "I've signed up for every spa treatment, culminating in the Salem Retreat, in which you're pressed beneath layers of hot rocks and ripe cranberries!"

"Sounds bewitching," Didi commented as she sorted toys. "But aren't we all going to be busy with our children?"

"Deed, that's what the Kidsatorium is for!" Betty reminded her. "Each morning we drop off the pups and head for the All-Day Breakfast Buffet." She licked her lips as she imagined it. "I hear they make a mean egg-yolk omelet. With five kinds of sausage."

Chas and Kira Finster—Chuckie and Kimi's parents—wore matching Hawaiian shirts as they checked their matching schedules.

"We signed up the kids for 'Pirate Play and Pillage' class," Kira told Didi.

"It teaches tolerance for the peg-legged," Chas added proudly.

Howard picked up a ten-pound hand weight. "Well, I'm going to use the whole seven kid-free days to reshape my physique," he announced. He tried to do an arm curl with the weight, but his arms were so skinny, he pitched forward onto the floor. Betty helped him to his feet.

"Could happen," she teased. "The Earth was created in six."

Stu bounded down the stairs, carrying baby Dil, whom he'd dressed in a little sailor hat. "Everyone all set?" he asked the grown-ups cheerfully.

Everyone spoke at once.

Didi clapped her hands to get everyone's attention. "I think we should all thank my husband, Stu, for arranging this wonderful getaway."

"No," Stu said modestly. "You can all thank me by having the time of your lives."

• • •

First the babies and their families flew on a big plane to southern China.

Then they got up early and hurried to a busy dock. Tommy looked around in amazement.

The boats tied to the dock were as big as hotels! Rainbow-colored confetti fluttered down from the sky. Crowds of people hugged and laughed and cried as they shouted "Good-bye!" and "Bon voyage!" to the people who were going away. It was like a birthday party for everyone!

Tommy and his family and friends waited in front of a huge boat. Dr. Lipschitz himself stood on deck and shouted to his guests, "Welcome aboard the world-renowned Lipschitz cruise!"

Tommy giggled in his mommy's arms. She was so excited, she was jumping up and down.

But suddenly the grown-ups all started to look worried. It was time to board the boat, but Stu had disappeared.

"Stu must have taken Spike for one last potty run," Didi said, looking around nervously for her husband and the family dog. "I'm sure he'll be right back."

"He'd better," Drew fumed, searching the

crowd for his missing brother. "He's got all our tickets."

To entertain the babies while they waited, three-year-old Susie Carmichael showed them what she'd brought on the trip. An instant camera! She took a picture—*snap!*—and then something wonderful happened. The picture popped out of the camera! The babies crowded around to marvel over Susie's magic.

"That sure is a nice cambera, Susie," Tommy said.

Susie smiled. "Thanks, Tommy. My mommy got it for me, so she and my daddy can see what they're missing while they're 'scovering diseases and stuff. But they really wanted me to come on this vacation with you guys, so—"

"And we're glad you did, Susie Carmichael!" Angelica said, butting in. She smiled brightly. She was dressed in a brand-new tropical-print outfit. And she was hiding something behind her back.

Susie blinked, surprised—and a little suspicious.

Angelica revealed what she'd been hiding behind her back: her favorite doll.

This time Cynthia was dressed in a sparkly dress with a long feather boa wrapped around her neck. The doll held a tiny microphone in her little plastic hand.

Angelica shoved a flashlight into Susie's hand. "Now, here! Hold the spotlight on Lounger Singer Cynthia!"

Then she held out a doll-size baby grand piano. With a grin, she pushed a button, and the tiny piano began to play a tune. Angelica made the doll dance in the air as she belted out a popular song, messing up the words as she went along.

Susie glanced sideways at Tommy. "I wonder if it's too late to call my mommy."

Meanwhile, Didi checked her watch.

Howard stared strangely at the cruise ship. "Is it me?" he asked the others. "Or is the dock moving?"

All the grown-ups looked around. Then they realized the dock wasn't moving—the boat was!

Just then the cruise boat blasted its horn. *Hooonnnnk! Hooonnnnk!* It was *really* time to go.

"The ship's sailing without us!" Drew shouted in alarm.

"Stu!" Didi called, searching the sea of faces in the crowd.

The babies' parents ran along the dock, shouting at the departing ship.

"Hold that boat!" Betty shouted. "There's a chafing dish full of pork with my name on it!"

"What about our 'Romance through Whale Watching' seminar?" Chas yelled.

"I really need to pump some iron!" Howard said.

"There must be some mistake!" Didi cried. "Dr. Lipschitz! Come back!"

The cruise ship blasted its horn once more, then slowly pulled away from the dock.

Didi, Drew, Charlotte, Betty, Howard, Kira, and Chas couldn't believe it—their vacation was sailing away!

CHAPTER 4

Seconds later everyone heard another sound: a weak little horn. *Honk! Honk!*

The grown-ups looked toward the sound. They couldn't believe their eyes.

There was Stu, wearing a captain's hat. And he was sitting at the wheel of a boat. Not a grand, luxurious yacht. Not even a charming midsize boat. But a shabby little boat with peeling paint, tied by a frayed rope to the dock. Beside him, Spike barked and wagged his tail.

"Ahoy, mates!" Stu shouted cheerfully. "Captain Stu, at your service! Climb aboard for seven fun-filled days on the SS *Nancy*. No fancy packaged tour. Just the thrill of the open sea, the smell of the salt air, and the joy of close friends and family!"

Stu's voice rang out across the dock. All the other vacationers had boarded the cruise ship, and their families and friends were heading home. The confetti lay trampled and dirty on the ground. A lone seagull squawked and flew off to find a better spot to hunt for food.

The Pickles party stood rooted to the dock, silent, their mouths hanging open in shock as they tried to make sense of what they were seeing and hearing.

Suddenly Charlotte snapped to life. She slipped out of her expensive pumps and shoved them into her husband's hands. "Drew, hold the shoes." Then she dived straight off the dock into the water and began swimming toward the SS *Lipschitz*.

• • •

A half hour later the SS *Nancy* churned through the waves with Stu at the helm. The angry grown-ups had bundled the babies in bright orange life jackets and corralled them in a makeshift playpen at the bow of the ship.

"Look at me!" Angelica shouted, the wind in her pigtails. "I'm queen of the world!"

"Isn't this a great bacation, guys?" Tommy said.

"As long as the 'queen' doesn't sing, I'm happy," said Susie.

"And the best part is, we're all togethers!" Tommy said.

But Chuckie was looking a little pale. "I likes the togethers part," he said, holding his tummy, "but this boat ride's making my tummy a little tumbly."

Lil pointed into the distance. "That's on accounta those really big waveses."

"It's just like my bathie!" said Phil. "Only there's no rubber ducky and I'm not nakie."

A white seagull floated by, riding up and down on a wave.

Susie snapped a picture.

"There's a ducky!" Kimi said.

Phil's eyes shifted back and forth, and then he shrugged. "Well, okay. Time to get nakie!"

He started to yank off his shirt, but his head got stuck. He couldn't see, and he fell over backward. Lil helped him up.

"And look," Kimi said, pointing at the grown-ups. "Our mommies and daddies are happy to be togethers too."

The adults had hauled Charlotte back onto the SS *Nancy*, and she'd changed into dry clothes. But she'd missed the real boat, and her face turned a bright red as she searched for her cell phone to call Jonathan and complain.

Kira clung to the railing, turning a pale shade of green.

Chas's face wasn't green—it was nearly purple. "I can't believe you did this without asking us!" he shouted at Stu. "Look at poor Kira! This was supposed to be our honeymoon."

Kira moaned and hung over the side of the boat as it bounced over the crest of a wave.

"Sorry, Chas," Stu said. "And here I was hoping you'd be my first mate."

"Me? Really?" Chas said, flattered. He'd never been a first mate before.

But Drew was not so easily swayed. "Snap out of it, Gilligan!" he shouted at Chas. "At the next port we're getting off this rinky-dink tub—and getting *on* the Lipschitz cruise!"

Stu was surprised by his friends' reactions. He tried to make them understand. "Don't you see?" he argued. "If we were on the cruise right now, we wouldn't be together! We'd be split up between the pools, the spas, and the mile-long buffet."

"But we're missing Canadian-Bacon Tuesday!" Betty complained.

Charlotte pounded the dashboard of the boat. "Can't this bait-trap go any faster?"

Stu's shoulders slumped and his smile drooped into a disappointed frown. This was not turning out the way he'd pictured it at all.

Didi was busy trying to get an old short-wave radio to work. "Hello? Hello? Is anybody there? Is this thing on?"

At last the radio crackled to life. And though the words were a little garbled, they could make out a familiar voice. *"Welcome, passengers, to what I like to call 'the voyage of your lifetime!'"*

It was Dr. Lipschitz himself!

"Everybody!" Didi called out. "I'm getting a signal! It's from the Lipschitz cruise!"

The grown-ups crowded around Didi as she frantically fiddled with the dials. There was more static, and then they heard a voice.

But this was not Dr. Lipschitz. This was a different voice. The voice of a teenage girl.

"Mom, are you there? I'm having a little trouble with the wild child."

The grown-ups looked at each other, confused.

"Sounds like a disgruntled passenger," Chas said. "I hope things didn't get out of hand at the 'Pirate Play Day.'"

Charlotte grabbed the microphone. "Hello, Lipschitz? Charlotte Pickles here. Could you send a rescue boat right away? We're the squalid little boat in the middle of the ocean."

•••

"Huh?" On an uninhabited island not too far away, a teenage girl sprawled on a lounge chair, with her lunch, a soda, and a shortwave radio on a table beside her.

It was Debbie Thornberry, daughter of

famous television naturalists and explorers Nigel and Marianne Thornberry.

In fact, she was trying to talk to her famous parents on the radio. But she kept getting a weird interference.

She stared at her sister, Eliza, who was eating at the picnic table. But Eliza just shrugged.

"Hang on a sec, Mom," Debbie said. "I'm picking up some lame-o soap opera." She turned the radio dials some more.

"What's the problem, Debbie?" Marianne asked.

"Okay, I made everyone lunch," Debbie began, "so I shouldn't have to clean up, too, right?"

"Can we talk about this when your father and I get home?" Marianne said.

"Yeah, any ETA on that?" Debbie asked. "'Cause you've been gone since, like, yesterday."

"We're still looking for the leopard," Marianne said. *"Oh! Nigel! Over there! What's that?"*

Debbie and Eliza could hear their father in the background. *"I see spots! Oof! Watch out for that limb, dearest!"*

Debbie and Eliza heard a clunk as if their mother had dropped the radio, then the sounds of two people running through the brush.

"Oh, it's gone!" Marianne exclaimed with disappointment.

"Here, Neofelis Nebulosa," said Nigel. *"Come to papa. . . ."*

"Hel-lo?" Debbie said grumpily. "I was talking here!"

Marianne picked up the radio. *"Sorry, Debbie. What were you saying?"* she asked.

"Let me talk to Mom," said Eliza, reaching for the walkie-talkie. But her sister held it away.

"No way!" declared Debbie. "Go pick fleas off the monkey."

"Mom!" Eliza yelled.

"Girls, don't fight," said Marianne. *"Now, you're on your own for dinner tonight. Why don't you make tuna noodle? All you have to do is add warm water."*

"Tuna noodle?" asked Eliza. "Again?"

"You know, normal families eat dinner together once in a while," said Debbie, sulking.

"Marianne!" interrupted Nigel. *"Perhaps I can lure out the leopard by imitating its mating call!"* Nigel proceeded to make a rumbling, growling sound.

"Okay, so we're not normal," admitted Debbie. "But as a teen, I reserve the right to alternately reject and embrace my parental units. You're the only family I've got and we're on a deserted island. When are you coming home?"

"Not until tomorrow morning," answered Marianne. *"Now keep an eye on Donnie. It's going to rain, and you know how he likes mud. Over and out."*

Debbie heard a click. "She totally hung up on me," she said sadly, staring at the walkie-talkie. "And I was having a sensitive moment."

"Debbie, you are so self-centered," said Eliza.

There was a crack of thunder, followed by a downpour of rain. Darwin began to chitter.

"I am not!" replied Debbie.

Then she stopped and looked at Darwin. "Okay, what's the monkey saying about me?" she asked.

Crack! A bolt of lightning lit the sky. Back on the SS *Nancy*, Stu cringed. They'd been so busy arguing, no one had seen the storm brewing.

Big fat raindrops splattered on the deck of the boat. And then the rain poured down as though a dam had broken in the sky.

"I hope it's not acid rain," Chas worried.

The wind howled as the ocean tossed the SS *Nancy* around like a toy boat in a baby's bathtub.

Together, Stu and Howard fought to hold the wheel. Drew struggled to tie down lines. The moms bailed water as it poured in an unending waterfall over the sides of the boat.

"Captain Stu!" Howard shouted. "I can't hold the wheel!"

"Move it down below!" Betty ordered.

"Will you stop calling him 'Captain'?" Drew protested angrily. "He has *no* idea what he's doing!"

"I do so!" Stu shouted back. Then he bit his lip. "Uh, does anyone know where the brakes are on this thing?"

A wave crashed over the boat, soaking Chas and draping him in a veil of seaweed.

"Jonathan!" Charlotte was shouting into her cell phone. "Why aren't you answering the phone? I need you to divert a tropical storm—"

She broke off as she stared ahead.

A huge mountainlike wave was headed straight for them!

"Oh, no! It's a forty-foot wall of water!" Stu shouted.

"We're gonna need a bigger boat . . . ," Chas said.

"Everyone get below!" Betty ordered.

As the grown-ups clutched their babies and scrambled down into the tiny cabin, something even more unthinkable happened to Charlotte: She dropped her cell phone into the ocean.

"Phone overboard, phone overboard! *Jonathan!*" she screamed. She lunged for it, but Drew grabbed her and dragged her below.

Stu was the last person on deck. He took one final look at the monster wave, then ducked down below and slammed the hatch.

Huddled with their children, the grown-ups braced for the blow. As the giant wave crashed down, the boat pitched and hurled through the water, tossing families around in the cabin.

The grown-ups screamed.

The babies screamed—in delight.

Unaware of the danger, Tommy and his friends laughed and squealed as if they were on a ride at the amusement park.

It seemed as if the storm lasted for hours, but at last it passed. The SS *Nancy* settled . . . upside down.

The table and chairs were now on the ceiling. The deck was below the cabin. Tommy thought it was funny. But the grown-ups didn't look very happy. They frowned and groaned and muttered as they untangled themselves and picked up things that had spilled across the cabin.

"*Mommy*," Angelica whined as she picked up her doll, "Cynthia's hairdo fell out!"

Charlotte hugged her daughter. "Mommy's got bigger problems right now, sweetheart." Then she turned to the others. "Somebody, do something!"

Everyone looked around, trying to figure out exactly what that something should be.

Chas noticed the hatch, which was now on the floor. "Well," he said, reaching for the handle, "this is how we came in. . . ."

"*Noooo!!!!*" the others screamed.

But it was too late. Chas had yanked open the hatch.

But since the boat was now upside down, the hatch didn't open toward the sky. It opened underwater.

Water sprayed into the ship as if from an opened fireplug.

"Why didn't anybody stop me?" Chas moaned.

Water began to fill the inside of the cabin, rising steadily over their feet, their ankles . . .

The grown-ups scooped their children into the air.

"Out of my way!" Charlotte shouted. She tore off her slim skirt, revealing some stylish shorts underneath. Then she quickly climbed the ladder. When she reached the top, she removed her shoe and pounded it against the ceiling that used to be the bottom of the boat. At last the wood splintered. As rain poured in, she tore away enough wood to make a hole big enough to climb through.

Everyone else crowded around the bottom of the ladder.

Kira made her way up the ladder with Chuckie and Kimi clinging tightly to her sides.

As the water rose higher and higher Drew helped Angelica and Susie climb to the top, then Didi, Tommy, and Dil.

Howard scurried up the ladder with the twins.

As the rest of the crew climbed the ladder Betty did something unexpected.

"Right behind you, boys!" she said. But she didn't climb the ladder. Instead, she took a deep breath, then dived beneath the water.

She swam, with open eyes, searching, searching . . .

There! At last she spotted what she was looking for: a yellow rubber square. She grabbed it. Then, almost out of air, cheeks bulging, she started to swim to the top.

But then she saw something important. Something they couldn't leave behind.

Without a second thought she dived back down to get it.

• • •

Up above, the rest of the soggy group clung to the hull of the overturned boat in the driving rain, gasping for air. *Where is Betty?* they all wondered.

A few tense moments later Betty broke the surface, gasping for air.

"I got it!" she cried, then proudly handed the small important item to Didi. "Dil's Binky!"

"Oh, Betty, thank you!" Didi managed a

shaky laugh and popped the Binky into Dil's mouth.

Then Betty held up the yellow square, which had a small cord dangling from one side. "I thought this might come in handy too."

She yanked the cord, and like magic, a large yellow lifeboat inflated to full size!

"Abandon ship!" Betty cried.

The adults eagerly climbed into the raft with their children. Didi had managed to snag Dil's stroller, and now she folded it up to almost pocket-size.

Stu grabbed the skipper's wheel as it floated by, then watched as the SS *Nancy* slowly sank forever beneath the ocean waves. "I can't help feeling partially responsible," he said with a sigh.

The other grown-ups glared.

Suddenly they heard a wonderful sound— barking!

"Spike!" Stu shouted.

The rain-drenched group broke into smiles as they watched Tommy's dog swim out of the wreckage.

"Here, boy!" Didi called.

As Stu pulled Spike into the lifeboat the overexcited dog bumped into Angelica. Cynthia tumbled from her hands and into the water.

Angelica shrieked. "Cynthia overboard!" She leaned over the edge to try to catch her, but Charlotte held her back.

"Cynthia!" Angelica screamed. "No . . . no . . . noooooo. . . ."

Sobbing, Angelica watched Cynthia sink below the water, weighted down by her tiny toy piano.

"There, there, Princess," Charlotte cooed. "We've all lost something today. Why, I lost my cell phone with one hundred free minutes, Daddy lost his favorite sun visor, and Uncle Stu lost all our respect. . . ."

Stu looked around at the others. Feeling miserable, he hunched down in his tiny corner of the lifeboat.

CHAPTER 6

The hot sun blazed down on a deserted white beach unspoiled by human footprints. Crabs skittered by, uninterested in the doll that lay half-buried in the sand, wreathed in seaweed, her microphone held high.

Suddenly a cry pierced the air.

"Cynthiaaaaaa!"

It was Angelica. She was the only one awake in the tiny lifeboat that drifted gently toward the shore.

She had just spotted Cynthia, so she scrambled over the babies, jumped from the boat, and splashed into the shallow water to rescue her.

Back on the lifeboat the babies woke up and looked around.

"That was a good nappie," Phil said, stretching.

"It was just like when Mommy used to rock us to beddie-bye," Lil said with a sigh.

Chuckie clutched his stomach and groaned. He looked a little green. "Well, I likes a bed that doesn't move."

Just then Spike leaped from the boat and went splashing through the water. His jumping jostled the small lifeboat, and the grown-ups slowly awakened.

Stu rubbed the sleep from his eyes, then burst into a grin. "Land ho! Land ho!" he shouted.

"What's happening?" Chas said, looking around.

Stu leaped into the water and used the rope to drag the lifeboat toward the sand.

Laughing in relief, the grown-ups gathered their children and came ashore.

"I'll never set foot on water again!" Howard vowed. He sank to his hands and knees and kissed the wet sand. The sand tasted terrible! He sat up and spat.

"Where are we?" Kira wondered.

"Oh, isn't it obvious?" Charlotte exclaimed happily. "The palm trees, the white sand, the crystal blue water . . . Why, we've landed on an island resort!"

Betty studied the deserted beach: She saw no people. No hotels, no shops, no restaurants. She shook her head. "This place looks pretty deserted."

"Oh, Betty," Charlotte said with a laugh. "The best ones always are. Just look for a cabana boy carrying towels. Hellooo!" she sang out. "I could use a double espresso, chop chop!"

Stu pulled something from his pocket. "Don't worry. I've got a map. We'll figure this thing out." The others gathered around as he unfolded the large map. "We left here. . . . We capsized here." Suddenly he grinned. "I know exactly where we are! See?" He pointed to a small scrap of land. "We're on this tiny little island called . . ." He squinted at the tiny type.

"Un-in-habited," he read, as if reciting a foreign language.

Didi gasped, and Stu realized what he'd said. *Uninhabited.* He glanced up at his friends. "Uh-oh."

"You mean we're the only people here?" Didi asked fearfully.

"Well, we'll just have to get back in the boat and row to another island," Charlotte said. "One with coffee." She whirled around and marched back toward the water. But then she froze. "Drew!" she shouted. "The lifeboat's gone!"

The grown-ups stared out past the shore. The lifeboat bobbed on the gentle waves as the tide carried it out to sea. They watched as a fat seagull landed on the side of the inflatable boat. It poked at the side with its beak.

"Nooo!" the grown-ups gasped.

But it was too late. The bird's pointed beak stabbed the rubber. Slowly the air seeped out. The lifeboat sagged and then sank beneath the waves.

Drew whirled on his brother, furious. "You didn't tie up the lifeboat?"

Stu cringed. "I meant to. . . ."

"We're marooned?" Howard shrieked. "With no food?" His eyes took on a crazed look. "I have to get out of here!" he shouted. Then he ran like a madman down the beach.

Betty shook her head. "Okay, so Swiss Family DeVille he's not."

CHAPTER 7

Nigel and Marianne staggered into camp, their eyes red from lack of sleep.

"Debbie!" Eliza called out, scooting into her seat. "They're here!"

With a yawn, Nigel sank down on the bench. He smiled and sniffed the wildflowers. "Ah, the *Dendrobium biloculare* orchid, discovered in Papua New Guinea in nineteen oh—"

Nigel slumped forward on the table, out cold.

"We were up all night looking for that leopard," Marianne explained over the snoring. Then she gently shook her husband's shoulder. "Honey, wake up."

Nigel startled awake. "Back, you four-toed beast!" he shouted. Then he shook the dream from his mind and remembered where he was. "Oh. Hello. Lovely to see you."

Debbie came out of the Commvee carrying a big surprise: a tray of juice, tea, and lumpy-looking muffins. She'd actually made breakfast.

"I hope you're all hungry. Homemade coconut muffins and herbal tea."

"Debbie!" Marianne exclaimed, clearly surprised. "This is so sweet!"

"I could use a spot of tea," Nigel agreed. He chose a cup and took a sip. "Oh, and these look heavenly," he said, referring to the muffins. "Afraid we must eat and run." Nigel gulped some tea and stuffed some muffins into his pocket. He stood up, ready to go.

"Well, Marianne, shall we return to our task?"

Marianne took a quick bite of her muffin and got up from the table.

"These are really delicious, honey," she said to Debbie. "Okay, I'm ready!" she replied to Nigel.

Debbie and Eliza looked at each other with dismay.

"But you guys just got here!" said Eliza.

"I know," said Marianne. "But the foundation is expecting that footage today, and we still haven't got it. Nigel, I think we should split up."

"Dearest!" Nigel gasped in alarm. "I thought we were so happy!"

Marianne rolled her eyes, and Nigel chuckled. "Oh, you meant to look for the leopard, didn't you?"

"I can't believe this!" cried Debbie. "You guys would probably desert your own children if some yellow-footed kanga-bear thing walked by!"

"Where?" asked Nigel as he and Marianne looked around excitedly.

"Oh, poodles. You're just teasing your old dad," chuckled Nigel. "There's no such creature."

"That's my point! You're always working. When's the last time we took a vacation?" asked Debbie.

"But Debbie, we travel all over the world," said Marianne. "Look—we're on a tropical island."

Debbie sighed. "Mom, please. How many white-sand beaches can a girl take? I want a family vacation. . . . You know—where we fight over the bar of hotel soap . . . and sing dumb songs in the car . . . and you make us do dorky family activities together!"

"That does sound really great!" said Eliza.

"See?" Debbie pointed out. "Even Nature Girl wants outta here! So just give me your credit card and I'll take care of everything."

"Honey, I'm sorry," said Marianne. "I didn't realize you felt this strongly. I promise, as soon as we find the leopard, we'll do dorky family activities."

"We'll tour the States in search of man-made oddities!" Nigel chimed in. "I hear there's a giant ball of baling twine in Ohio."

"Even that sounds good," said Debbie. "And it wins the Lamest Idea Ever award."

"Thank you, poodles," Nigel chuckled. "It's settled then."

As Nigel and Marianne took off, Eliza gathered her things and put them in her knapsack.

"You're leaving too?" asked Debbie sadly. "Fine, go. I was gonna hang out on the beach today anyway."

"Debbie, are you forgetting that I talk to animals?" asked Eliza.

"Sadly, no," replied Debbie. "Your point?"

"I'm gonna find out where that leopard is, so we can leave," explained Eliza. "And then maybe we'll really take a vacation. But we have to talk Dad out of that baling twine thing."

Debbie smiled.

"Come on, Darwin!" called Eliza.

Darwin was sitting on the lounge chair in a floppy flowered hat and oversize sunglasses, dabbing white sunscreen on his nose. The girls stared at him. Darwin held a magazine upside down in front of his face and chattered wildly.

"Darwin's staying here," Eliza translated. "See ya." Then she hurried off.

Donnie rushed past Debbie using a paddle to whomp muffins into the air. A pair of birds swooped down. Donnie jabbered in delight as one of the birds caught a muffin in its beak.

"Donnie!" Debbie protested. "I did not slave over a hot oven to feed the birds!"

Donnie dropped the paddle and disappeared into the bushes.

Debbie sighed. "When I write about my life—and I *will*—I will not be kind."

•••

Still believing they were alone on a deserted island, Tommy's parents and their friends gathered driftwood and built a playpen as the babies toddled around, wiggling their toes in the sand.

Betty forced a big smile for the children. "Okay, kids. You play here while the mommies and daddies try to ward off the specter of doom." Then she rejoined the grown-ups. Now that their children were safe and tucked away, they could try to come up with a plan for getting home.

"Babies, listen up," Angelica announced as soon as Betty was gone. "We're stuck on a top-ical island that don't got no people on it!"

The babies looked at her, confused.

"But *we're* here, Angelica," Kimi pointed out.

"I mean people who *matter*!" Angelica declared. "And we gots no food! And no cookies!"

Phil patted his diaper with confidence. "Puffy, don't let me down."

Angelica fumed. "I'm not talking 'bout your moldy crumbs, DeVille. Those aren't gonna last the rest of our lives."

Susie scoffed. "You don't know what you're talking about, Angelica."

"Oh, yeah? I saw a movie 'bout it once." Angelica leaned forward and spoke in a spooky voice. "These little kids were all alone on an island till they growed up and turned wild. The boy grew a beard down to his feet, and they had to wear rags for clothes!"

The babies gasped.

Angelica smiled—now she had their attention! "But that's not the worstest part," she added with a sly smile.

The babies held their breath—what could be worse?

"There are giant mutant lobsters on the island!" Angelica revealed.

"No!" said Susie. "It's not true—"

"Yes, it is!" Angelica insisted. "And there's only one way for you to survive: You must obey *me*—'cause I'm the Island Princess now."

Now the babies knew what could be worse than being stuck on a deserted island:

Being stuck on a deserted island with Angelica!

The hot sun beat down on the grown-ups. Their throats were parched. They were starting to panic.

And they'd only been on the island about an hour.

"It's obvious," Stu was saying. "The first thing to do is make a signal fire."

"You know what *else* is obvious?" Drew snapped, kicking sand at his brother. "You're an *idiot.*"

"Without my SPF 115, this tropical sun will render me unconscious," Chas said nervously. "You really should go ahead and vote me off this island now."

"Oh, Chas," Kira said. "We would never do that."

"Yes," Charlotte agreed. "We have bigger problems than a little sunburn. We must focus on our basic needs. Like checking e-mail. Ideas, anyone?"

"Well, at least we have one meal," Didi said. "I saved a couple of jars of baby food."

Just then Howard joined the group, his mouth rimmed with something green and orange as he used his finger to scoop the last dollop of goop from several empty baby food jars. "Mmm," he murmured. "I never knew strained peas and apricots went so well together."

"Howard!" Kira exclaimed in shock. "You ate the baby food?"

"Babies don't need food!" Howard argued. "I have to keep my strength up for when you try to throw me in the soup pot!"

"He's delusional," Didi whispered to the others.

"Phobias are a terrible thing," Chas pointed out. "We mustn't blame Howard."

"Oh, we're not blaming *Howard*," Drew said, glaring pointedly at Stu.

One by one all the grown-ups turned toward Stu.

Stu took a step back.

"This is all your fault!" Drew shouted.

"*My* fault?" Stu said.

"Whose idea was the Stu Cruise to Doom?" Charlotte demanded.

"I would expect that from the Finsters or the DeVilles," Didi said, defending her husband, "but Charlotte!"

"That's *not* very nice!" Chas protested.

Drew shook his finger at Stu. "I've known this day was coming since you were in diapers!"

"I should never have left Paris!" Kira moaned.

The quarrels grew louder and louder.

Finally Betty stepped away from her bickering friends. She picked up a stick. Then, without a word, she began to draw.

One by one her friends fell silent as they watched her draw a line in the sand. The line grew and curved until at last, when she was finished, it encircled them all.

"This is the Circle of Chaos," Betty announced. "If we're gonna survive on this island, we can't ever step foot in the Circle of Chaos."

Her friends looked down at their feet, then quickly jumped *out* of the circle.

"Wow. I feel calmer already," Chas said.

"People," Betty said in her strong, confident voice, "we don't know when we'll get off this island. And until we do, we're going to need *order*."

Everyone nodded in agreement.

"First thing we need is a leader," Betty added. "Any volunteers?"

Stu eagerly raised his hand.

Didi cringed. She knew the others probably wouldn't vote for her husband if he was the last candidate on Earth. "Stu," she whispered gently, "put down your hand."

Charlotte's hand shot up. "I nominate Betty."

"I accept," Betty instantly replied. "All in

favor of me, raise your hand."

Everyone raised his or her hand.

Everyone but Stu. "Hold on," he protested. "You're all going to blindly follow Betty just because she drew a circle in the sand?"

"Yes!" they shouted.

"Thank you," Betty said. "As my first duty as your rightfully elected leader, I'm assigning Stu to baby-watch. The rest of you, follow me."

Betty handed her stick to Howard and marched off down the beach. The others followed without question.

Didi glanced back over her shoulder at Stu. She shrugged apologetically, but then followed Betty and the rest of her friends.

Stu's shoulders sagged in defeat as he turned back toward the playpen. With a sigh, he plopped down in the sand. "All I wanted to do was have a little adventure. Now everyone and their brother is blaming me for this mess."

Inside the playpen Tommy watched his father in dismay. "Angelica, are the growed-ups mad at my daddy?"

"That's a blunderstatement," Angelica said.

"He's in *big* trouble. It's 'cause of him we're gonna hafta live here forever."

Tommy thought about that for a moment. "Maybe we can help."

"You babies are gonna help?" Angelica laughed hysterically. "Ha! You can't keep your fingers out of your nose."

Tommy pulled his toy binoculars from his diaper. "We gots to try, Angelica." He peered through the cracks of the playpen. "Guys, I see something! I think it's the topical drain forest—just like we sawed on Nigel Strawberry's telabision show!"

The babies eagerly gathered around.

"Does that mean Nigel Strawberry's there?" Kimi said.

"What makes you think that big-nosed nature guy's on this dinky island?" Angelica said.

"Because that's the lastest place we saw him," Tommy explained. "He was getting eated by a crockagator."

Phil snickered. "Nice knowing you, Chuckie."

"Phil!" Chuckie shrieked.

"I bet if we go in there, we'll find him," Tommy said. "And my grampa said Nigel Strawberry can get out of any trouble. He can help us get home!"

"And no one would be mad at your daddy no more!" Susie said.

"And I wouldn't hafta share the waffle I gots in my diapie!" Phil said.

Everyone looked at Phil.

Lil elbowed Phil in the ribs. "Phil-ip."

"Uh, if I *had* a waffle in my diapie," Phil sputtered.

But Tommy had more important things on his mind. "Who wants to go look for him with me?"

"Me!" said Kimi.

"Lead the way, Tommy!" said Lil.

"Let's get out of here," said Susie.

"No waffles here," Phil said.

"Well, there's the bald leading the bald," Angelica said.

Tommy just ignored her and led the babies out of the gate. Susie snapped a photo as she pushed Dil's stroller past Angelica. "See you, Angelica."

Angelica couldn't stand it when the babies ignored *her* and followed Tommy. "Hey! You babies hafta stay here and start being my royal subjects!"

They ignored her.

"I'm warning you!" yelled Angelica. "Those giant mutant lobsters eat babies with a side of butter!"

The babies kept toddling.

"Get back here!" she commanded.

But Tommy and his friends never even looked back as they disappeared into the forest.

"Tinkleheads," she muttered.

Meanwhile, Stu had wandered down the beach in search of driftwood. So he never noticed when the babies broke out of the playpen.

"I'm going to build a signal fire that will have us off this island in no time," he said with renewed confidence.

Stu turned his pockets inside out. All kinds of junk tumbled out. "Let's see," he said as he picked through the jumble. "Gum . . . my special 'writes upside down' pen . . . a disposable razor. . . ." He sighed. "Great. I can chew, shave, then write about it . . . on my head," he muttered miserably when he realized he had no paper.

Angelica spotted her uncle and marched up to him.

She stared at the stuff scattered all over the sand. "What's all this junk?"

"It's not junk, Angelica," Stu replied. "These everyday items can be used to make lots of things."

Then something happened in Stu's brain—in the part that loved to invent things.

"That's *it*!" he cried. "I'll build a radio and send a distress signal!" He patted his niece on the top of her head. "Angelica, keep an eye on the babies for a minute, okay?"

Then he scooped up his things and ran off before she could say a word.

"But they went off into the drain forest!" she shouted after him. But she could tell he didn't hear her. Grown-ups never paid attention when it was really important. "Great," she muttered. "Now *I'll* get in trouble when those dumb babies get losted."

She stomped over to Spike, who had dug a little hole in the sand and was curled up in it, napping. She gave him a poke. "Spike! Wake up! Go get the babies. I got important things to do. Like find someone to be my royal subjects."

Spike sniffed. He sneezed. He chewed at some fleas on his rear end. Then he yawned and went back to sleep.

Angelica fumed and stomped her feet. Then she wandered down the beach. At least she had *one* friend who would always listen. "Cynthia, this vacation stinks! I been walking forever and no one's come along to carry me yet!"

She glanced up at the sky and spotted something strange. A pair of birds—and one of them had a delicious-looking muffin in its beak.

"Hey! That bird's got a cupcake! Drop it, Beakhead! Or else! Hey! I said, *or else!*"

The bird cawed, pooped on Angelica, then flew away.

"Yuck!" Angelica squealed, and wiped off her clothes. "There's gotta be someone else around here I can boss."

Then she heard a funny noise from behind a rock. Angelica's eyes lit up.

She crept up to the rock and peered around it.

She'd stumbled upon some kind of camp with a huge van parked in the middle. And there, stretched out on a lawn chair, was a baby-sitter-type girl. She was tall and slim with long, wavy blond hair, sunglasses, and a bored-looking scowl. A small table beside her held a soda, a tray of snacks, and a boom box.

But strangest of all . . . a little gray chimpanzee wearing a blue-and-white-striped tank top and blue shorts was painting her toenails while he gobbled Cheese Munchies.

The chimp chattered wildly at the girl.

"Listen up, monkey," the girl said in a bossy tone of voice. "All that chimp chatter really bugs me. Just hand over those munchies and keep fanning."

The girl yanked her headphones on and grabbed the bag of snacks.

Angelica had no way of knowing it, but that snotty girl was Debbie Thornberry. And the chimp was Darwin, her sister Eliza's best friend.

Angelica was fascinated. "Wow. She's got that monkey waiting on her hoof and mouth," she whispered to Cynthia. "I could learn a lot from that girl."

Shyness was never one of Angelica's qualities. She marched over and stood in front of the girl. "Excuse me," she blurted out. "Miss Bossy Lady?"

The chimp stared.

But Debbie's sunglasses and headphones kept her from seeing or hearing Angelica.

Angelica swiped the palm frond from Darwin.

The little chimp shrieked.

"Pipe down, monkey!" Angelica told him. Then she whipped the palm frond back and forth and shouted at the girl, "Hey, lady!"

Debbie sprang from her chair. "Who's calling me a lady? I'm a teen!" She ripped off her sunglasses and stared down. A little girl with blond pigtails stood in front of her, whining about something.

"Where'd *you* come from?" Debbie asked. "This is supposed to be a deserted island."

Angelica rolled her eyes. "I'm Angeli-tiki. The Island Princess. And I'm thirsty." She plopped down on Debbie's chair, grabbed her soda, and slurped down the last drop.

"And," Angelica added, wiping her mouth with the back of her hand, "I lost my touch for being bossy. So you gotta teach me."

She leaned back in the lawn chair and held out the glass. "No ice cubes next time," she announced grandly.

Debbie just stared at Angelica. She'd never seen anything like her.

Darwin couldn't take it. One bossy, bratty human girl was difficult enough—two would be unbearable. Chattering frantically, he ran off into the forest. If he was lucky, he'd get hopelessly lost and never see either one of them ever again.

Tommy Pickles and his friends were all set to board a cruise ship, but they ended up on a small, run-down boat!

When their boat was hit by a storm, they found themselves stranded on an island . . . and then their wild adventure began!

The parents and babies thought the island was deserted, but it turned out that the Thornberrys were there too! The babies set off to look for **Nigel Thornberry**.

"NIGEL STRAWBERRY CAN HELP US GET **HOME!**"

Phil tried to grab a quick snack, but Lil's bug-eating days were over.

"Let him **go**, Phil!"

While looking for Nigel, Chuckie got lost and ended up switching clothes with Donnie Thornberry!

Susie caught all the action on film! "Say, 'Cheese!'"

Eliza Thornberry and her pet chimp, Darwin, met Tommy's dog, Spike. Eliza offered to help Spike look for Tommy and the other babies.

"Thank you!" said Spike. "That is so nice!"

During their search they met Siri, a fierce clouded leopard. Eliza's parents had been looking for a clouded leopard for days!

"A small chimp for **breakfast**, a mutt for **lunch**, and a sensible girl for **dinner!**"

"SNIFF MY **BUTT!**"

On another part of the island Angelica stumbled upon Debbie Thornberry. But when Angelica found out that Siri was going after the babies, she used the Thornberrys' bathysphere to rescue them.

With Angelica in charge of the controls, the bathysphere plunged to the bottom of the ocean!

"I NEED A **REFILL**, EXTRA ICE, **TWO STRAWS!**"

Marianne Thornberry used Stu Pickles's coconut radio to contact Nigel and the babies. With some teamwork, everyone was saved! Soon they were able to get off the island.

Tommy and his friends had expected to go on a luxury cruise, but instead they had gone on a wild adventure. Not bad for a bunch of **babies**!

CHAPTER 9

Off in the drain forest Tommy Pickles led his tiny band of loyal followers toward adventure.

Beneath a thundering waterfall, they oohed in delight as the sun painted a rainbow through the sparkling water.

As they headed deeper into the tangled forest they marveled at all the colorful birds, lizards, and other animals they saw. It was like a zoo with no cages.

Kimi loved the beautiful flowers, and she stopped to smell them as they hiked along.

Chuckie liked flowers too, so he copied his sister and bent down to smell one.

Just then a big bug fluttered by and—

Chomp! The flower devoured it!

Chuckie shivered.

Suddenly Phil spotted something fascinating: a millipede crawling on the ground. He picked it up and held it before his eyes. "Look. It's got a gazillion feets." He grinned. "Well, down the hatch!"

Lil's eyes flew open. She stared at her twin brother, who was dangling the millipede over his mouth. "Philip! No!" she shouted, reaching for the bug.

"Oh, sorry," Phil said sheepishly. He held it out to his sister. "Want a bite?"

"No!" Lil exclaimed. "I don't think we should eat bugs no more."

"That's crazy talk, Lil," Phil said. "We've been raised on bugs."

Lil's face twisted into a sad pout. "That's afore I sawed that poor fly get eated by that flower. . . ." She frowned at her brother. "Now, let him go," she ordered.

Phil looked at the bug. He looked at his sister and knew better than to argue. With a sigh, he put the leggy bug on a leaf and watched it crawl away.

"Bye-bye," Dil babbled.

"If I knowed the last bug I eated would be the last bug I eated, I woulda eated it slower," Phil said sadly.

Tommy was busy studying some muddy footprints. "Guys, look!" he called to his friends. "Growed-up feetprints! I bet they're Nigel Strawberry's! Let's go!"

Tommy pointed toward the direction where the footprints disappeared deeper into the forest.

Susie and the other babies eagerly followed. This was even more fun than playing Nature TV at home.

A few moments later Chuckie came out from behind the tree, pulling up his pants. "You know, it's a lot easier going potty in the drain forest than at home. And you don't hafta worry 'bout getting any on the floor or the walls or the—"

Chuckie's head whipped around. "Guys? Wait up! Uh . . . guys?" He could hear all kinds of strange noises: squawks and caws and hums and groans.

But not a single word of baby babble.

His friends were gone. He was all alone . . . in the drain forest!

Chuckie ran. But only because he was too scared to stand still.

CHAPTER 10

Eliza Thornberry was up a tree, trying to help her parents find that rare clouded leopard to film for their nature program.

Her parents were using their nature skills and experience in tracking animals.

But Eliza was using her special skill. A skill her world-famous parents couldn't even dream of: her ability to talk to animals. She couldn't tell her parents about it. But she *could* use it to help them.

"Excuse me," Eliza said to a slow loris who was dangling from a limb. "I'm looking for a clouded leopard. Have you seen any around?"

"Sure," the loris said. "There's one at the—"

"Eliza!" Darwin shouted as he swung by on a vine. "You'll never believe what I just saw!" He disappeared into the leaves. "Run along, little loris," he scolded. "This is a family matter. Scoot!"

"Hey," the loris protested. "Just because I'm small doesn't mean——"

Then he spotted something on the ground: Spike was sniffing at his tracks.

"I mean, sure thing!" the loris exclaimed as he swung off through the trees. "Family matter. None of my beeswax. *Bye!*"

Eliza sighed.

Meanwhile Spike was sniffing the roots of the same tree. He selected a good spot and lifted his leg.

Eliza began to climb down, still frustrated because the loris had run off. Suddenly she froze. "Darwin, look!"

Eliza climbed down to investigate.

"Uh. Hey. Hey. Could you give a dog a little warning?" Spike barked as she and Darwin reached the ground. "I'm trying to do my business here."

"Oh, I'm so sorry," Eliza apologized.

Spike stared at Eliza and cocked his head to one side. How curious. She actually *understood* what he said. Most people—no matter how much he barked or growled or whined—never seemed to understand a word he woofed. He laughed.

"You know, it's funny. For a minute there I thought I actually heard you talking to me. . . . You talking to me? . . . Are you talking to me?"

"Yeah, I can talk to animals." Eliza shrugged. "It's a long story. Should we come back?"

"Ah, no problem. I'm done. I was just marking." He looked around and barked, "Spike was here!" Then he smiled at Eliza. "I am sorry. Where are my manners? I'm Spike. Full name— Down Spike."

Eliza giggled. Darwin rolled his eyes.

"I'm Eliza. And this is Darwin."

Spike sneezed on the chimp.

"Spike was here, too," Darwin said in disgust, wiping his arms.

"Wow! I've been sneezing all day," Spike

said, shaking his head. "My sniffer's on the blink. Can't even smell my own butt. And let me tell ya, I've tried. Would you believe I can't smell a thing?"

"Charmed," Darwin drawled sarcastically.

"Spike," Eliza asked, "what are you doing here?"

Spike hung his head, embarrassed. "Well, eh, I'm . . . to be honest with ya, I'm looking for my babies."

"You lost your babies?" Eliza exclaimed.

Darwin whispered to Eliza, "Probably too busy drinking from the toilet."

"I was not!" Spike protested. "I was sleeping, okay?"

"That was my second guess," Darwin said dryly.

"Hey, smart boy! You don't get it, okay?" Spike said, sinking down on his haunches. "This is how it works. Usually, they wander off, I find them, no problem. But I can't smell! I might as well not even call myself a dog." Spike sat down and hid his face between his paws.

Eliza climbed down to pet him. "Don't

worry, Spike. We'll help you find them." Eliza scratched the dog's head, then whispered, "And I won't tell anyone you lost them."

"Really? You will really help me find them?" Spike wagged his tail. "Thank you! That is so nice." He jumped up and—*slurp!*—licked her face.

Eliza giggled.

Darwin shuddered. "Animals!"

CHAPTER 11

Near the center of the island, a sleeping volcano reached toward the sky. Tommy led his small band of babies up the steep slope. I bet we can sees the whole world from the top, Tommy thought. And maybe Nigel Strawberry, too!

Behind Tommy, Susie pushed Dil in the stroller. Phil, Lil, and Kimi lagged behind.

Suddenly Phil turned around, and Lil saw that there was a worm in his mouth.

"Philip, no!" cried Lil. "We don't do that no more!" She grabbed the tiny bug and tenderly placed it in her pocket.

"Aw, just one little wormie, Lil, please?" Phil pleaded. "Don't you 'member how good they used to taste? How they tickled on the way down?"

"No, I don't," Lil said firmly. "I told you—I'm a vegetableatarian now. We don't eat bugs— we pet 'em."

Phil looked horrified. "I don't knows you anymore, Lil! Do you still like to eat mud?"

"Not if it has a face," Lil replied.

"But you're my twin!" cried Phil. "Who's gonna do that stuffs with me anymores? And who's gonna tell me when my feet smell?"

Suddenly Dil giggled and banged his rattle. Phil smiled.

"Thanks, Dilly," said Phil. Phil plopped down, pulled off his shoes and socks, and then held his feet up to Dil. Dil sniffed Phil's feet.

"Stinky!" declared Dil.

"Okay, Dil. Do your stuff," instructed Phil.

Dil giggled and licked Phil's feet.

Suddenly Kimi looked around, worried. "Guys, I haven't seen Chuckie for a long time."

"We better go back," Susie said. "You know

how scared Chuckie is of being losted—"

But then Dil banged his rattle on his stroller and shouted: "Chubby!"

The babies turned around.

Donnie Thornberry stood at the edge of the forest. His hair looked wild and messy. He was wearing Chuckie's glasses and his clothes.

The babies thought he was Chuckie!

Donnie jabbered wildly as he raced over to Dil's stroller. He took a bite out of the baby's pacifier and stuck it back into Dil's mouth.

Then he leapfrogged over Phil and landed in front of Tommy. He grabbed Tommy's binoculars and stared in the wrong end.

"Or not," Susie said, astonished at the change that had come over their shy friend Chuckie.

Tommy looked at his friend in dismay. Was Chuckie sick? He never acted like that! "Uh, is everything okay, Chuckie?"

Donnie hollered out sounds that made no sense and signaled for the others to follow him. Then he darted into the forest.

The babies looked at one another, puzzled.

"When did Chuckie start talking back-ward?" Phil asked.

Tommy didn't know what was going on. Chuckie was always a good follower. Maybe it was time to follow him for a change.

CHAPTER 12

Nigel Thornberry was doing what he loved best: finding animals with scientific knowledge.

But no matter how hard he searched, the leopard still eluded him. "Not a hair. Not a pawprint. Not even a dropping!" he said, exasperated. But then he pulled his socks up. "Must keep a chin up. I'll find that cat, or my name's not Nigel Archibald Thornberry—"

Suddenly he heard jabbering in the bushes.

"Donnie? Is that you?" He scanned the jungle with his binoculars. He saw a tiny person with shoes. But that was puzzling. "When did Donnie start wearing shoes?"

At that very moment Tommy was staring

through *his* binoculars. And when he spotted Nigel Thornberry, he did a double take. Then he began to babble a happy greeting.

"Great Goodall!" Nigel exclaimed. "A baby!" And then he saw that there was more than one. "A *gaggle* of babies! What are they doing here?"

He started toward them, still watching them through the binoculars. "Children!" he called. "Stay right there! I'm coming down!"

Still looking through the binoculars, Nigel took a step and fell over the side of a cliff.

Luckily he was able to grab hold of a tree root.

"Not the way I intended . . . ," he mumbled. He noticed two birds nestled in a crevice in the cliff. "Ah! A red-footed booby . . . appears to be enjoying a coconut muffin . . ."

Just then the tree root gave way. Nigel plunged down the side of the cliff. He lay motionless at the bottom.

A few moments later Nigel sat up slowly and shook his head.

"Heavens, what a fall!" But then he remembered. "I must get to those babies." He stood up, but a falling coconut struck him on the head and knocked him back down.

Nigel rubbed his head. He felt dizzy and dazed.

"Ouchie!" Nigel said, his mouth crumpling into a pout. "I want my mumsy!"

Tommy couldn't believe it. He'd found Nigel Strawberry, only to see him fall over a cliff. He and his friends raced over to see if he was all right.

"Are you okay, Mr. Strawberry?" Susie asked.

Nigel stood up, a bit unsteady on his feet. But then he waved at the babies and snickered. "She called me 'mister'! Silly billy. I'm only this many years old!" Nigel babbled, holding up three fingers.

The babies looked at one another, confused.

"Do any of you remember where I left my tricycle?" Nigel asked, looking around.

"Uh, no, Mr. Strawberry," Susie answered. "We're shipwrecked on this island. We were hoping you could help Tommy's daddy."

But Nigel seemed not to understand the

question. "Watch what I can do!" he exclaimed. "Oopsie-daisy!" And he stood on his head.

"Why's he doing that?" Susie whispered to Tommy.

"Uh, well, maybe that's how he figures out where he is," Tommy suggested.

A bird landed in front of Nigel's upside-down nose. Nigel tumbled out of his pose. Frightened, the bird flew away.

Nigel chased it, flapping his arms. "Come back, birdie-wirdie!"

Susie turned to Tommy, confused. "Tommy, I think Nigel Strawberry's acting kinda funny."

Nigel skipped by like Goldilocks on the way to visit the three bears.

"Maybe he's got diapie rash," Lil suggested.

Nigel began to spin, his arms stretched open wide. "I'm a ballerina!" he shouted to the sky.

Phil gave a low whistle. "That rash is gonna need extra oinkment."

• • •

Chuckie nervously tiptoed through the woods. He was still trying to find his friends. "Tommy? Kimi? . . . Anybody?"

No one answered.

Then he heard strange jabbering sounds above him.

Hunching his shoulders, Chuckie slowly looked up.

A group of lorises sat in the trees, chattering loudly.

"Oh, no," Chuckie moaned. "Not mokeys!"

Chuckie ducked into a hollow tree. Then he peeked out.

A group of big lorises was chasing a little one. The little one had a piece of fruit.

"Hey, they're chasing that little one!" Chuckie muttered. "That's not very nice."

Forgetting how scared he was, Chuckie crawled out of the tree.

The lorises saw him and froze.

The little one darted behind Chuckie. The other lorises gathered around him, their large round eyes staring at him.

"Now you big mokeys go 'way," Chuckie said nervously. "You was little mokeys yourself once. . . . Um, probably. So just go 'way and leave this mokey alone."

The lorises stared.

Chuckie timidly raised his arm a little. "Shoo . . . shoo . . ."

To Chuckie's surprise, the lorises scattered.

The little one dropped the fruit at Chuckie's feet, then ran off, too.

"Thanks!" Chuckie picked up the food. Then he smiled. "Wow . . . I saved someone 'stead of someone saving me. I must be a wild boy now."

Chuckie toddled onward. He'd never felt so brave in all his life.

CHAPTER 13

Eliza was crawling on her hands and knees. *Sniff! Sniff!* She was following Spike's directions, sniffing the ground, trying to smell what he normally could. But her human nose just couldn't work as well as a dog's.

"Catch a whiff of anything yet?" Spike asked.

"Just her dignity as it flies out the window," Darwin quipped.

"Sorry, Spike," Eliza said as she sat down on the ground. "But everything smells pretty much the same to me."

"Humans!" Spike exclaimed. "How do you live?"

"Well, Eliza, this is a new low," Darwin said. "Crawling around on the ground, acting like a dog. There's a good chance you'll get fleas." Feeling itchy just talking about it, Darwin began to scratch behind his ears.

Suddenly—

"Growl!"

A female clouded leopard announced herself and pounced to the ground just inches from Spike's stuffy nose. Snarling, the big cat bared her sharp, dangerous teeth.

Spike reared back, astonished. "Whoa, big cat! Guess I won't be chasing you behind the couch, eh, toots?"

Eliza gasped at the sight of the big cat circling Spike. "Ohmigosh. You're—"

"I am Siri," the animal declared. "The clouded leopard."

"I'm Spike," said the dog. "The purebred mutt!"

"Look at my claws," Siri snapped, her voice full of challenge.

"Sniff my butt!" Spike yapped.

Darwin jumped behind Spike. "Are you mad?"

"I was being social," Spike whispered.

"Of course," Darwin said sarcastically. "A simple handshake wouldn't do."

"I don't shake with cats," Spike said. "If you get my drift."

Siri slowly crept forward. "Now . . . a small chimp for breakfast, a mutt for lunch, and a sensible girl for dinner . . ."

Darwin screamed.

"Aw, chimpboy, don't worry," Spike said. "I know all about cats, with a capital *K*. Sit on a windowsill. Hack up a furball. Yeah, that's ferocious," he scoffed.

"Spike," Eliza warned, "this isn't your regular house cat."

"Look, they all twitch their whiskers one whisker at a time," Spike said, "just like you and me." He turned back to the snarling cat. "I can't sit around here howling with you all day, knucklehead. I gotta go find my babies."

Siri's eyes glinted with sudden interest. "Helpless offspring?" she purred, pretending to care. "Alone in the forest?"

"Yeah! Yeah! That's it! That's it! Have you

seen them?" Spike asked. "Little ones, walk on two feet? Last time I saw them, they were on the beach walking—stumbling, actually."

"*Two* feet?" Eliza said.

"Yeah," Spike replied. "They're my human babies."

With a growl Siri bounded into the forest.

Eliza whirled around. "I thought you were looking for puppies!"

"Oh, no. My pups are home with the wife. She can't travel. Delicate stomach. Me, I could eat anything. I ate one of Chuckie's diapers one time, and let me tell ya, *that* is spicy."

"Spike!" Eliza cried. "Siri's going after the babies!"

Spike realized his mistake. Siri was going after the babies, all right. But not as a favor. She was hunting for a good meal!

"Come on," Eliza called. "We have to find my parents!"

"When will I *think* before I bark?" Spike exclaimed as he chased after Eliza.

"Face it," Darwin said as he hurried to keep

up. "You have a tail. Evolution never gave you a chance."

• • •

Meanwhile, on another part of the island the grown-ups were hard at work.

Betty had totally gotten into her new job as tribal leader. She had streaked her face with red, and now she squatted in the sand pounding rocks together, making something.

Didi watched her nervously. "Betty, I know you're our leader. But I don't see how pounding rocks and streaking your face with war paint is going to help anything."

"Aw, Deed, it's just a little pomegranate juice." Betty stood up and fit a sharpened rock onto a bamboo pole. She'd made herself a primitive spear. Then she waded into the surf and stared down into the water.

Didi followed her. "What are you doing?"

"Going fishing," Betty replied, as if she did it every day. "Kira, whip up some fruit tartar sauce."

"Betty, no!" Didi protested. "We can't stoop to that. It's so primitive."

"Primitive?" Betty said. "Stop squawking." She shook her spear at Didi. "Betty no like!" She jabbed her spear into the water. And when she pulled it up again, a fish squirmed on one end. "Well, that was easy," she said, marching out of the water.

• • •

Farther down the beach Chas and Drew waded through the surf, gathering broken pieces of the SS Nancy, which had washed ashore.

Suddenly Chas's eyes lit up and he lunged for something in the waves. "The wheel from the SS Nancy!"

"Grab it!" Drew said enthusiastically. "We can build a waterwheel! Those shipwreck movies always have waterwheels!"

"Good thinking, Drew," Chas said. "Ooo! Milk!"

"Where?" asked Drew.

Chas grabbed a bobbing plastic milk jug. But before he could examine it, Betty ran up and snatched it from his hands. "Chas! As your leader, let me be the first to examine that."

She swiped her hand across her brow, and

accidentally smeared the milk jug with the red juice. It looked like a crude face.

"Empty," Betty said. "Don't people know better than to pollute the ocean? It's killing the fish!" With a grunt, she tossed the jug back into the water and picked up her spear.

Drew and Chas watched the bottle bob back out into the ocean.

"It almost felt like we found a friend," Chas said.

"It was two percent," said Drew.

"Farewell, Two," Chas said. "Safe journey!"

• • •

Elsewhere on the island Chuckie was wandering around alone, totally lost. He heard a strange jabbering and shivered.

"Who's that?" Chuckie said. "Phil? Lil? Uh—Spike?"

Chuckie ran off the trail, hoping to find a friendly face. But then he tripped on a root and fell facedown in the mud. He picked himself up with a groan. "I knew we shoulda stayed on the beach."

Chuckie toddled over to the lagoon to wash

off the mud. But when he looked at his reflection in the smooth surface of the water, he gasped. He didn't look anything like he did in the mirror in his bathroom back home.

His face and clothes were covered in mud. His glasses sat crookedly on his nose. His red hair was messy—even messier than it usually was.

He started to dip his hands into the water to wash them, then froze when he again heard that strange jabbering sound.

Chuckie's lip quivered as he gazed into the water. "I'm just a fraidy-cat Finster. A filthy, dirty, fraidy-cat Finster."

At least he could do something about the filthy, dirty part. He tugged off his muddy sneakers and socks and laid them on a rock. Then he pulled off all his other clothes till he was down to his underwear.

Cautiously he dipped a toe into the lagoon. The water was dark and cloudy. He couldn't even see his toes!

He knew Tommy wouldn't be scared. So he tried to think of Tommy as he waded in.

Nothing swam around his ankles. Nothing nibbled his toes. So far, so good.

Chuckie dunked his shirt and shorts up and down in the water. When his clothes looked pretty clean again, he spread them neatly on a rock to dry.

Then he tried to wash all the mud off his face and hands. But he splashed water all over his glasses. So he took his glasses off and carefully laid them on the rock beside his clothes.

Without his glasses, the world looked soft and fuzzy.

Suddenly he heard a voice humming a strange song.

Chuckie swallowed. "Phil?"

Silence.

Chuckie's knees began to quiver.

Then the humming began again.

"Lillian!" Chuckie shouted. "This is not funny!" He whirled around.

Across the lagoon he saw a boy standing in the water. Chuckie couldn't see him well without his glasses.

But he could tell a few things about him.

The boy was about his size.

He wasn't wearing a shirt, either.

And he had wild, messy hair.

Who was he?

Frightened, Chuckie took a step backward.

The other boy took a step backward.

Chuckie turned sideways.

The boy turned sideways.

Chuckie spun around and stuck his hands out. Ta-da!

The boy copied his motions.

Chuckie sighed in relief. It wasn't a real boy after all, he realized. "Oh, you're just my 'flection! How ya doin', Chuckie!"

The boy jabbered some words that made no sense.

Ooh! Chuckie clamped his hands over his eyes. "My 'flection never talked back! I been ascared of lots of stuff afore, but I never been ascared of me!"

Chuckie uncovered his eyes and blinked.

His "reflection" had disappeared.

"Hey! Where'd it go? Um . . . Chuckie?"

Chuckie still thought it was his reflection.

What he didn't know was that it was Donnie Thornberry. Donnie looked an awful lot like Chuckie. He wore nothing but leopard-print shorts.

Donnie crept along the bank of the lagoon, hiding from Chuckie. He scooped up Chuckie's clothes and glasses, then ducked behind a bush.

Chuckie waded out of the water, annoyed that his reflection had disappeared. "That's not very nice," he called out. "From now on I'm not gonna make funny faces with you no mores!"

Behind the bushes Donnie pulled off his shorts. Then he took his shorts and flung them over the bush.

Chuckie was feeling around the rock for his glasses and clothes when Donnie's shorts hit him in the face.

"Hey!" Chuckie shouted. "Who's throwing stuff?"

Donnie snickered in the bushes, but didn't answer.

Scowling, Chuckie picked up Donnie's

shorts and slipped them on. "Hmm," he said. "My shorts feel kinda big. . . ."

Behind the bushes Donnie had put on all of Chuckie's clothes. He put on the glasses and reeled a little as he got used to the way they made the world look, then steadied himself. He tossed the socks, but stuck his feet into Chuckie's sneakers . . . just as Chuckie discovered they were missing. "Who took my shoeses?" he demanded.

Donnie liked his new things. He didn't want to give them back. He started to sneak off, but tripped on the shoelaces. So he reached down, tied them into perfect bows, then ran off.

"Come back!" Chuckie shouted. "I won't hurt you!"

But the boy ran away anyway.

All alone, Chuckie scratched his head. Something really weird was going on. But he wasn't quite sure what. It was hard to think without his glasses on. Everything seemed fuzzy, even the thoughts in his head.

Sighing, he looked back at the lagoon and saw his real reflection in the water: a wild-looking boy with messed up, mud-streaked hair. And no clothes except a baggy pair of shorts.

Chuckie yelped. "I don't even look like Chuckie no mores. What are my friends gonna say?"

Then he gasped. "Angelica was right. This place *is* making me wear rags and turn wild!"

• • •

While her parents struggled, Angelica was having a marvelous vacation. She had made herself at home at the Thornberry camp, and was well on the way to twisting Debbie Thornberry around her little finger.

Lying on Debbie's lounge chair, Angelica lifted her sunglasses to look at the tray of cookies Debbie held out in front of her. Angelica picked three and stuffed them in her mouth. "These are much better than the cookies we gots back at the grass hut . . . and I don't hafta share with no dumb babies—I mean, dumb baby savages!" She slurped loudly from a juice box.

"Tell me about it," Debbie replied. "I have to share with a pigtailed weirdo, a jungle freak, and a monkey in a tank top."

Debbie slurped the remains of her soda and handed the glass to Angelica. "Refill," she demanded.

"Why do I hafta get it?" asked Angelica with a scowl.

"You said you wanted to learn how to be bossy, right?" answered Debbie. "This is how you learn. Extra ice, two straws."

With a frown Angelica went inside the Commvee.

Debbie chuckled to herself. "I'll trade the monkey for her any day."

Suddenly the walkie-talkie on the table crackled to life. *"Debbie!"* Marianne called. *"Come in. Over."*

Debbie picked up the walkie-talkie. "Hey, Mom," Debbie said. "How's it going?"

"No luck," Marianne responded. *"Have you heard from your father?"*

"No, but get this, Mom—"

"Tell me later, honey," Marianne said. *"Be back soon."*

Angelica looked around inside the

Commvee. "Angeli-tiki is nobody's slackey," she said to her doll.

Angelica kicked a hatch in the floor of the Commvee. She opened it and discovered a strange bubble-shaped vehicle not much larger than a gorilla's cage.

"Hey, lady, what's that bubble thing?" Angelica called out.

"A bathysphere," Debbie shouted back. "It goes underwater. You know, like a submarine. Getting thirsty here!"

"That girl's even bossier than me," Angelica muttered. She walked toward the refrigerator when a glint of light caught her eyes. "What's that light?" she wondered aloud.

Just then she spotted a pair of binoculars on the table. She picked them up and looked outside.

In the far distance Angelica spotted a volcano rising into the sky.

But just then something was traveling up the side. Babies!

"Those dumb babies are practically on top of a mountain, and *I'm* gonna be blamed! I gotta go home and pretend I'm innocent." She rushed out and threw open the Commvee door.

"Um, Debbie? I just 'membered . . . I was supposed to be home for, uh, the Island Sacrifice!" she fibbed.

"Okay. My mom will drive you when she gets here," Debbie said.

"But I hafta go *now*!" Angelica shouted. "I'm the princess. Who do you think's gonna throw in the goat?"

Debbie hesitated. "Oh. Okay. It's a native thing. Mom will understand. But I'm not waiting around to watch the goat bite it."

Debbie climbed into the driver's seat of the Commvee, and Angelica hopped up on the seat beside her.

Debbie glanced at Angelica.

Angelica impatiently buckled herself in, then pulled down the sun visor. Then she used the power switch to lower the window. "Is that a CD player?" Angelica asked.

"Yeah, only the best." Debbie slid in a CD, then glanced sideways at her passenger. "You know an awful lot for an 'island girl.'"

"Um, well, see, a TV washed up on the

beach once. And the Island King made the whole tribe watch it."

As the CD kicked in, a popular tune blared out of the speakers.

"I love this song!" Angelica exclaimed.

"Hey, me too!" Debbie said.

Together the girls sang along as the Commvee made tracks along the beach toward the ancient volcano.

Suddenly three figures burst out of the forest. Debbie swerved to miss them. The Commvee spun out in the sand and headed straight for the lagoon.

Angelica covered her eyes.

Thinking quickly, Debbie pulled a lever marked BOAT MODE. Instantly, some pontoons inflated on the side of the Commvee as it splashed into the water.

Debbie looked out the window to see who she'd almost hit.

It was her sister, Eliza, along with her crazy monkey pal Darwin and . . . a dog.

"Debbie!" Eliza shouted as she ran toward the Commvee "There's a bunch of babies lost around here, and the leopard's after them!"

Angelica gasped. "I didn't know there was a leopard out there!" she muttered to herself. "If Drooly loses a piece of ear, I'm gonna be in big trouble!" She yanked off her seat belt and ran to the back of the Commvee. "I've got to get out of here!"

Angelica looked for a way out. Then she remembered the hatch. "C'mon, Cynthia. We're taking a ride!" Then she disappeared down the hatch.

"Angeli-tiki!" Debbie called.

She opened the hatch and looked. Then she slammed it shut. "Oh, man. Not the *bathysphere!*"

Suddenly the floating Commvee jolted as the bathysphere shot out from beneath it. As Angelica escaped, she struck one of the pontoons on the Commvee and punctured it.

Water poured into the Commvee through the gash in the side. Debbie looked around. All of her things started floating out the open windows. "My stuff!" she shrieked.

The Commvee was sinking!

CHAPTER 14

Eliza, Darwin, and Spike rushed over to the side of the lagoon.

"Debbie!" Eliza called. "What happened?"

Debbie appeared at the window—which was now just inches above the water. "I was taking care of this island princess, and—"

Just then the bathysphere bobbed to the top of the water—with Angelica at the wheel.

"What's she doing in the bathysphere?" Eliza exclaimed.

Debbie shrugged. "I didn't say I was taking care of her *well*."

Angelica waved at them, then yanked a

lever. The bathysphere disappeared beneath the water.

"Don't worry about that one," Spike said. "She's feisty. I've seen her bite a monkey's tail."

Darwin was shocked. "I knew that girl was trouble!"

"Hey, you should see her with scissors and a doll's head," Spike confided. "Oh, boy. And I've seen that kid eat her weight in paste—"

"Spike?" Eliza interrupted. "The babies. Come on."

"Right," replied Spike. "Babies. Let's go!"

• • •

Nigel was teaching the babies how to play follow-the-leader. He led them up a hill.

Nigel hopped. "I'm a kangaroo!"

The babies all hopped behind him.

Then Nigel flapped his arms. "I'm a vampire bat!"

All the babies flapped their arms.

Then Nigel leapfrogged. "I'm a froggie!"

The babies leapfrogged after him.

Phil stopped and adjusted his diaper. "All this hopping is making my diapie creep."

But now Nigel had stopped, too. He stared with childlike wonder at something off in the tangled jungle. "Ooo, now I'm a giant kitty cat!"

But this time it wasn't pretend. This time something very real *growled*!

And then Siri, the clouded leopard, crept toward them, baring her teeth.

The babies huddled in fear. But Tommy tried to reassure them. "Don't worry, guys. Nigel Strawberry plays with wild aminals all the time. He'll get us out of this scrape!"

Nigel stepped closer to the wild animal. "Does kitty want a mousie?" Nigel asked. "Does kitty want to dress up in dolly clothes and take a ride in Nanny's pram?"

Nigel tried to pet the leopard. But the wild cat swiped at him with her paw.

Stunned, Nigel looked at his hand. Then his face crumpled. "Kitty gave me a boo-boo!"

Siri sensed that the adult human was no

longer a threat and turned toward the babies, her eyes gleaming.

The babies were so scared they couldn't move.

But Donnie had grown up in the jungle and had learned to be quick. With a shout he pulled Dil from his stroller. Then he picked up the stroller and jabbed it at the leopard as if he were a lion tamer in the circus.

The babies were amazed—they still thought this strong, brave boy was their old fraidy-cat friend Chuckie.

"Chuckie!" Kimi warned. "Be careful!"

"He's so brave!" Lil sighed.

"Or dumb," muttered Phil.

Donnie shouted wild things at the leopard, then finally set the stroller on the ground. He motioned for the babies to get in.

"Everyone, climb on!" Tommy commanded.

But Nigel shoved his way to the front. "Me first, me first!" With a whoop he dived into the stroller before anyone else. His long legs and arms dangled over the side.

Quickly Tommy and his friends piled in. Then Donnie took a flying leap and jumped on.

The babies squealed as the stroller shot down the hill—with the leopard right behind it.

But suddenly Donnie saw something off in the forest. With a shout he jumped off the stroller.

"*Chuckie!*" the babies cried as the stroller rolled on down the hill.

Donnie did a few wild somersaults, then landed, face-to-face, with the real Chuckie.

"I been looking all over for you," Chuckie scolded Donnie. "I don't like being half nakie. I want my clothes back."

Chuckie didn't know that Siri was slowly creeping up behind him.

Donnie jabbered and yanked Chuckie into a thick tangled thicket. The bushes shook as he traded clothes.

"Hey!" Chuckie cried. "I gots sticks in my hair! I gots no shoeses! Ow! My feets!"

All the while the leopard prowled around the thicket, searching for a way in.

At last the real Chuckie came out. He was wearing his own shirt and his own shorts, but he was still barefoot. And he'd gotten his glasses back. He put them on and smiled. The fuzzy world went away. Now he could see everything, sharp and in focus, including Siri.

"Ahhhhhh!"

Donnie leaped to Chuckie's side, grabbed a huge palm frond, and laid it on the ground. Then he shoved Chuckie down on it and gave him a big push.

Chuckie went flying down the hill as if he were sledding on snow.

Donnie made faces at the leopard. He shouted at it and threw sticks, trying to attract its attention.

But nothing worked.

The leopard ran after Chuckie.

Down below the babies watched in horror from the racing stroller.

"Hurry, Chuckie!"

"C'mon!"

Nigel giggled as if it were all a fun game. "Next stop—Piccadilly Circus!"

The leopard ran closer and closer. Then it sprang toward Chuckie!

Tommy grabbed his best buddy and pulled

him into the stroller just in time. Susie snapped a picture for her scrapbook.

The stroller continued to fly down the hill over bumps and turns.

At last the leopard gave up the chase.

Tommy and his friends sighed in relief. They were safe!

But then the stroller headed toward the mouth of a cave and disappeared.

Inside it was dark and spooky. Strange rock formations rose like statues in the dim light. The stroller hit a bump, throwing Nigel and the babies down a dark tunnel.

The tunnel was a little like a waterslide and a little like a haunted house—fun and scary at the same time. The babies screamed as they slid through the dim light. Bats flew out of the shadows. Critters skittered along the walls. Twigs snatched at their hair and clothes.

At last they arrived at an underground lake and landed with a thud on the shore.

They all looked at Nigel, who was splashing playfully at the water's edge. "Look, Mumsy!" he shouted with glee. "I'm a whale!"

Chuckie gasped. "That's Nigel Strawberry!"

"Are you sure he can really help us?" Susie whispered to Tommy.

"Acourse he can," Tommy said. "He's Nigel Strawberry. He's the bestest Nature 'splorer ever." Then he added sadly, "Or . . . I thoughted he was."

The babies sat down on the little patch of beach. They began to think about their mommies and daddies.

"Guess we're stuck here till somebody finds us," Lil said sadly.

"Who's gonna find us here?" Kimi said.

"I know what will cheer everybody up," Phil said brightly. "A nice waffle." He dug into his diaper and pulled out his last half-eaten waffle. It was a little mashed from being sat on, but the babies were so hungry, they didn't care. Phil divided it up, square by square, and handed each friend a piece.

"It's kinda crusty," Lil complained as she took her share. "You gots any mabel syrup in there?"

Phil checked his diaper. "Nope." He held up some tiny packets. "But I gots some ketchup."

Nearby Nigel was making faces and blowing spit bubbles at Dil, who was propped up against a rock. "Watch this one!" Nigel said. He twisted his face into a goofy expression.

Dil giggled and drooled.

Susie shook her head. "Maybe telabision people are only good at doing stuffs on telabision," she said quietly.

"Well, I guess we'll be living on this island from now on," Lil said in a quivering voice.

Susie choked back a sob. "That means . . . I might not see my family again for a long time. . . ."

Phil leaned toward her. "Uh, are you gonna eat that waffle?"

"Shh, Philip," Lil said in a loud whisper. "Susie's sad."

"I'm sad, too," Kimi sniveled. "I want my mommy and daddy!"

Susie started to cry. Then Kimi started to cry. Then Phil and Lil began to cry.

Chuckie sniffled, trying to hold back his tears. "I'm feeling kinda scared, too."

The sound of his fellow babies crying broke

Tommy's heart. "I'm sorry, guys," he told his friends. "I never shoulda broughted you here. Angelica was right. I *am* just a backyard baby with a diaper full of dreams."

One by one the babies stopped crying. They looked at Tommy in surprise.

"No, you're not," Susie said, wiping her eyes. "Tommy, you took us through the drain forest all by yourself!"

"And led us up the side of the mountain!" Kimi said through her sniffles.

"And you founded Nigel Strawberry," Phil pointed out.

"And you saved me from the giant kitty cat!" Chuckie reminded him.

"Oh, you got *lots* more than dreams in your diapie, Tommy!" Phil pointed out.

Everyone stared at Phil.

He shrugged. "What?"

Tommy checked his diaper. Then, finding everything in order, he stood up. "Thanks, guys. That's the nicest stuff anyone's ever said. So even though we're stucked in a cave and there isn't any boat and we can't swim, I promise to get you outta here!"

"All right!" Phil shouted.

"Yay, Tommy!" cried Lil.

"You can do it!" Kimi told him.

"Go, Tommy!" Susie cheered.

Tommy continued. "It's like my hero Nigel Strawberry always says—"

"The Martians have landed!" Nigel shouted.

"Uh, no," Tommy said. "I was thinking 'bout when he says, 'Don't give up hope, fateful viewers!'"

"Welcome to our planet," said Nigel. "How many eyes do you have?"

The babies turned to Nigel. He was standing on the edge of the shore, waving and pointing at something in the water.

Something was rising out of the water. And it did look like a Martian spaceship.

Angelica Pickles popped out of the hatch of the Thornberrys' bathysphere and waved like a beauty queen. "Adoy, babies! Look what *I* got! *Now* who's your princess?"

Tommy groaned. He just hoped his mommy and daddy found him soon.

CHAPTER 16

The grown-ups weren't looking for their babies. They still didn't know they were missing. They were busy trying to make houses and find food. It looked like they were going to be on this deserted island for a long, long time.

They had built several bamboo huts. Chas and Drew were on top of one, adding large, thick palm leaves for a roof.

Charlotte walked by, an orchid pinned behind her ear. "Drew, there's no longer a ringing in my ears from constant cell-phone usage. Isn't this paradise?"

Drew smiled. "Sure is, honey." He turned to

Chas. "Hand me that frond, would you, neighbor?"

"Well, technically, this is a Finster frond," Chas said, reluctant to share, "because it's dense enough to block even the strongest ultraviolet rays. But to show goodwill, I'll donate it to your roof." He paused, then added, "As long as I can stand in your house at high noon."

Farther down the beach Kira had been collecting coconuts and had piled them up in a long wall. "One hundred and fifty-two coconuts. This should last through winter."

"Sure," Betty said. "And it makes a nice barricade if pirates ever attack."

Betty strode toward the water's edge, where her husband, Howard, was turning a fish on a spit over a fire. Didi was using a small rock to chop seaweed and arrange it on large shells she'd found to use as plates.

"Didi," Howard said, pointing at the fish, "do you think this is done? I've never cooked a fish with its head still on."

"Well, let me see . . . ," said Didi. "Does it flake when you touch it?"

Suddenly Howard shrieked, "*My fish!!!*"

Everyone looked back at the fire. The fish was gone.

Even stranger, a small wild-looking boy sat on a rock by the fire—with the tail end of the fish sticking out of his mouth. He blinked at the grown-ups staring at him, then swallowed.

"No, no, no!" Howard shouted, rushing over. "That's my fish! *Give it back!*"

The boy jabbered wildly.

"Howard," Didi said, "he's just a little boy. Where do you think he came from?"

"I don't know," Chas said anxiously. "But those look an awful lot like Chuckie's sneakers."

Howard gasped. "Cannibal! You ate the fish *and* Chuckie!"

The boy was Donnie Thornberry, and he was still wearing Chuckie's shoes. He didn't like the way Howard was shouting. So he ran away and disappeared behind a sand dune.

The group exchanged a look. Then—

"After him!"

"Catch him!"

"Hurry!"

"He's getting away!"

• • •

Not too far away on another stretch of beach, Marianne Thornberry had set up a tripod to film some sea turtles who were digging nests in the sand.

"Well, it's not a clouded leopard," she muttered to herself, "but at least I'll have film of *something*."

With a sigh, she peered through the camera's viewfinder to set up her shot.

Something streaked by. And it definitely wasn't a turtle!

She looked up and saw an amazing sight— her adopted son Donnie being chased by a mob of grown-ups!

"What the—? Donnie!" she shouted. *"Cut!"*

Everyone froze. They stared at Marianne in shock. Another grown-up! And she looked civilized!

Charlotte sank to her knees in the sand. "Thank heavens! We're part of an elaborate television stunt designed to humiliate us!"

"Uh, I think you have the wrong idea," Marianne said politely. "I'm Marianne Thornberry."

"From television?" Didi asked. Then, realizing who she was, Didi explained to the others. "She's Nigel Thornberry's camerawoman-wife!"

Didi then turned back to Marianne. "I read about you in a magazine last time I was at the dentist. We're shipwrecked, you see, and—"

Just then Donnie streaked across the beach.

"Cannibals!" yelled Howard. "I knew it!"

"Oh, no. That's just our Donnie," explained Marianne.

"And that's just our Howard," chimed Betty. "Can you help us, Marianne?"

Marianne pulled out her walkie-talkie. "Debbie? Come in."

The radio crackled to life. *Mom. What's up?*

"I need you to bring the Commvee over to the east beach."

"Uh, that may be a problem," Debbie said, hedging.

"Don't worry about cleaning up," Marianne said.

"Thanks. But that's not the problem—"

"Just get here. Now. Over and out."

Marianne clicked off. "My daughter will bring our trailer," she told the ragged band of castaways. "And my husband will be along soon. Don't worry. He's a very capable man."

"Someone talking about me again?"

Everyone turned. But it wasn't Marianne's husband. It was Stu Pickles, and he was carrying a strange device. It looked like a coconut that had been rolled through the trash.

Just then he saw their visitor. "Oh. Now who are *you*?"

"This is Marianne Thornberry," Didi said. "She's going to help us get off the island."

"Well, thanks," Stu said politely, "but there's no need, because I—Stu Pickles—have built us a radio!" He presented his invention with a flourish.

But as Stu showed off his invention, Didi realized her husband was all alone. "Stu?" she asked nervously. "Who's watching the kids?"

"Oh, Angelica said she'd take care of them," he answered absently.

The parents stared at him open-mouthed.

Then they rushed toward the now-empty pen where they had left their children that morning.

The parents started to panic.

Debbie, Eliza, Darwin, and Spike arrived on the beach just as a strange crackling static came from the coconut radio.

Marianne pushed toward her daughters. "Girls, have you seen some children?"

"Well, uh, just a bossy four-year-old who has delusions of being a princess," Debbie said.

"My baby!" Charlotte shouted.

"It's getting a signal!" Stu cried. He dialed the gold coin, trying to get a clearer signal as the other grown-ups gathered around.

At last they could hear voices.

"I'm the boss of this bathy thing, so listen up!"

"That's her!" Debbie shouted. "She must have turned on the radio in the bathysphere."

"A four-year-old's driving the bathysphere?" Marianne exclaimed in disbelief.

"You're not going to sing, are you?"

"That's Susie!" Didi yelled.

"Okay. It's no problem. We can track them by radar from the Commvee," said Marianne.

"Uh, yeah." Debbie studied a strand of her long blond hair. "Except . . . I sunk the Commvee."

• • •

Nigel and the babies were crammed into the bathysphere. Angelica and Susie were at the controls, trying to figure out how to make it go.

Angelica was driving—or at least, pretending to.

"I'm beginning to think you tooked this scrubmarine without permission, Angelica," Susie complained.

"Carmichael, nobody likes a backstreet driver." With a scowl, Angelica studied the control panel. All the buttons looked the same to her. "Now, here's the right button." She poked it.

The bathysphere didn't move. But an over-head compartment popped open, and a snorkel mask dropped down. Angelica quickly put it on. "Uh, here's the *other* right button. . . ."

With a jolt the bathysphere shot out of the lagoon and out to sea—right past their parents. The adults looked on in shock.

"What are they doing?"

"Who's driving?"

"Stop that bubble!"

"Nigel's with them!" Marianne said, trying to keep everyone calm. "We've got to try to reach them on your coconut. Can it transmit as well as receive messages?" she asked Stu.

"It's supposed to," Stu replied. He jiggled some wires.

"Uh-uh, Carmichael. She really did give me a cream soda."

"Girls! Girls!" Drew shouted, trying to make them understand. He sighed in frustration. "They can't hear me!"

Charlotte grabbed the coconut. "Angelica! Stop fighting this instant and listen to your father." Then she handed the coconut to Drew.

There was a moment of silence.

And then . . .

"Sorry, Mommy."

The grown-ups cheered.

"I'm very impressed," Marianne told Stu.

. . .

Inside the bathysphere the babies heard their parents cheering.

"Our mommies and daddies!" Tommy shouted.

"Daddy!" Angelica shouted into the microphone. "Tell Susie to stop bothering me while I'm trying to drive a scrubmarine."

"Give me that, Angelica." Susie grabbed for the mike and accidentally bumped the wheel. The bathysphere made a hard turn.

Nigel tumbled to the floor, and the babies scattered to get out of his way. As he fell, a small tin fell out of his pocket.

"What's this?" Nigel said as he picked it up. "A new toy?" He used the little key to roll open the can. A horrible fishy smell filled the cabin. "Oh! Kippers!"

The babies made faces at the awful smell.

But Nigel was delighted. He loved the tiny smoked fish.

"I'm the happiest lad in all of England!" he exclaimed.

"*Listen, Angeli-tiki,*" Debbie called over the radio. "*Let me talk to my dad.*"

"Hey, mister!" Angelica poked Nigel in the stomach. "Stop eating those smelly fish and talk to the lady!"

But Nigel was too busy playing with his food. "This little fishie goes to market. This little fishie gets eaten by Nigel the Giant."

• • •

Standing on the beach, the grown-ups stared at the sounds coming out of the coconut.

Debbie rolled her eyes. "Great. Dad finally lost it."

Marianne turned to the other grown-ups with a worried look on her face. "Something's wrong with Nigel."

Then she spoke into the radio. "Girls, this is Mrs. Thornberry. Do you see a red handle? I need you to push that up. That will bring you up to the surface."

"I see it!" Susie cried.

"Drooly, don't touch that!" Angelica shouted.

Suddenly, Dil pushed a lever—the wrong lever—and the bathysphere plummeted down to the ocean floor.

• • •

Dil clapped his hands as the bathysphere spiraled down into the darkest depths of the ocean. The babies shouted and hung on to one another.

Nigel was thrown against the wall. He hit his head *hard.*

At last the bathysphere landed with a thud on the ocean floor. The radio crackled once, then fell silent.

Just then Tommy noticed his hero lying in a crumbled heap. "Oh, no! Nigel Strawberry!" He rushed to his side. He pulled a baby bottle out of his diaper. "This calls for my 'mergency bottle."

He squirted milk in Nigel's face.

Nigel sputtered and opened his eyes. He sat up and wiped his face. Then he slowly rubbed his head and blinked.

The first thing he saw was Tommy's big smile. The first thing he heard was Tommy's baby talk. He couldn't understand a word.

"Hello, there," he said pleasantly. He stood up and looked around. "Well, what have we here? Who are all you positively adorable children?"

"We're shipwrecked," Susie said. "We went all over the island looking for you—"

"*I* saved them," Angelica interrupted, "but then Carmichael tried to drive this tub-boat, and now—"

"We just want to go home," Susie finished.

"Well, of course you do, young lady," Nigel said. "And so you shall."

Nigel walked over to the bathysphere's control panel and studied the readings. *Oh, dear!* he thought. But he tried to hide his concern from the babies. "Hmm . . . a bit of a pickle," he said to himself. "No fuel left. The radar appears to be knocked out, which means I have no idea where we are, and we're almost out of oxygen. . . ."

Angelica tugged on Nigel's sleeve. "I'm bored."

"Yes, and there's that, too," Nigel said.

"*Angeli-tiki, come in!*" Debbie's voice came over the radio. "*What's going on down there?*"

"Deborah?" Nigel said. "Is that you?"

"*Dad!*" Debbie cried. "*You're back to normal! Well, Dad-normal, anyway.*"

...

Up on the beach, the grown-ups gathered around Marianne as she spoke into the radio.

"Nigel, thank goodness you're all right," Marianne said. "Can you bring her to the surface?"

"*Impossible at the moment, dearest,*" Nigel said. "*You'll have to engage the automatic-retrieval system in the Commvee.*" Nigel lowered his voice. "*And I don't want to alarm anyone, but we're a tad low on oxygen down here.*"

"No air?" Kira cried.

"We have to get to them!" Didi exclaimed.

"Copy that," Marianne said to Nigel, trying to remain calm. "We'll get you out as soon as we can. Over and out." She handed the radio back to Stu. "We have to raise the Commvee."

Together Marianne and Betty waded into

the water to the cheers of the other parents. Then they disappeared beneath the water and swam toward the Commvee, which was wedged between some rocks. Marianne inspected the damage to the pontoon. Then she shook her head and gave Betty a thumbs-down signal.

"No go," said Marianne after they emerged. "The pump's destroyed. Plus there's a huge rip in the pontoon."

"Hang on," Drew whispered. "The Professor's getting an idea."

Everyone turned to look at Stu. He was drawing like mad on a large rock—wild sketches of scientific-looking diagrams and mathematical formulas.

CHAPTER

18

Up on the beach Stu called everyone to join him. Then he pointed a bamboo stick at his drawings. "Okay, here's the plan," he said. "With the energy from the bicycle-powered bellows . . ."

He pointed his stick down the beach. Eliza and Darwin sat on a pair of bicycles made from sticks and spare boat parts.

". . . air will be forced into the reeds . . ."

Air pumps on the bicycles were connected to hollow grass reeds lying in the water.

". . . which you gentlemen will connect with the deflated pontoons . . ."

Drew, Howard, and Chas stood at the

water's edge, ready to dive. They were connected with a rope, like mountain climbers on a safety line.

". . . which will force the Commvee out of the water once it is counterweighted with coconuts," Stu said at last.

Kira, Charlotte, and Didi were lined up on the beach to pass coconuts to Marianne and Betty near the edge of the lagoon where the Commvee was sunk.

"Any questions?" Stu asked.

"It's perfect," said Marianne. "But we still have to repair the pontoon or it won't inflate."

Spike and Eliza were a short distance away. "What's going on?" asked Spike.

"We can't raise the Commvee! We need something to patch the pontoon," Eliza explained.

Meanwhile, Debbie was standing in the water when she saw a torn yellow lifeboat.

"Eliza, come here!" Debbie yelled as Eliza and Spike raced down the beach. "There's a rubber raft out there. Can we use that?"

"That's perfect!" Eliza exclaimed happily.

But as Debbie tried to wade into the water to grab the raft, a huge wave knocked her down. The raft floated further out to sea.

"She found your boat, Spike!" Eliza explained. "They can use it to patch the Commvee!"

"I used to run with a buddy named Patch," Spike said. "Nice dog, black ring around his eye . . ." Then he realized what Eliza was saying. "Wait! Will this save my babies?"

"Yes," Eliza told him.

Spike growled. "I'll get it," he said.

"Spike, no!" Eliza begged. "The current is too strong!"

"Hey," he said, "this is Spike you're talking to! I've paddled my way to more tennis balls than I can count!" He blinked. "If I could count."

"I'm afraid you won't make it," Eliza said.

"Sure I will," said Spike. "And if I don't, well, no one's gonna say Down Spike didn't try his best! You only go around once in this crazy life. . . ." Then he stopped to think. "Well, not cats," he went on. "They get nine lives while dogs have to cram seven years into one human year. That's messed up. . . ."

"My babies!" he suddenly remembered. "Gotta go! Thanks for everything, kid!" And he leaped into the water and paddled against the waves after the raft.

Everyone from the other side of the lagoon ran to Eliza's side.

"Spike's swimming toward the lifeboat!" Didi said, amazed.

"Unbelievable," Marianne whispered. "It's as if he knows we need it to patch the pontoon."

Spike dog-paddled hard for the raft. Again and again the waves rolled him over. He came up a final time—with the raft's tow rope in his teeth.

Everyone cheered. Spike turned around and fought his way back to the beach.

"Good boy, Spike!" Stu cried. The dog dropped the raft at his feet.

Stu took out his pocket razor and cut a rubber patch out of the raft. Then Debbie rushed over and spat out a wad of chewing gum. She stuck the piece of gum onto the rubber and headed for the Commvee.

"I'll take care of it!" announced Debbie.

"Debbie?" called Marianne.

"Mom, don't argue with me," Debbie replied firmly. "You're exhausted."

"That gum won't stay sticky for long!" Stu warned.

Debbie ran into the water and dove in. She swam down to the Commvee with the piece of raft.

Underwater, Howard, Chas, and Drew fit the reeds into several places in the pontoon. Slowly, the pontoon began to inflate. Marianne and Betty lashed some coconuts to the side of the Commvee, and it began to tilt.

Stu checked his watch. "Any second now . . ."

Suddenly Debbie emerged from the water, gasping for air. She gave Stu a thumbs-up.

"Done!" Debbie announced as Howard, Chas, and Drew also popped up.

"I think I swallowed an entire ecosystem!" said Chas.

Stu waded into the water and observed the

Commvee. "Just ten more rotations ought to do it!" he called to Eliza.

Donnie pedaled furiously to raise the Commvee.

"Go, Donnie, go!" called Eliza.

Everyone watched as the side of the Commvee rose out of the water.

"Bingo!" shouted Stu.

"It's working!" cried Kira.

• • •

Down in the bathysphere Nigel was trying to keep the babies calm and entertained. He was singing to the tune of "Old MacDonald Had a Farm." But he was singing his own version:

"And on his farm he had a ring-tailed lemur . . ."

The babies were enjoying themselves, except for Angelica, who was bored. Suddenly, the lantern battery flickered.

"Oh, not to worry, children," Nigel reassured them. "Just another part of our little adventure, eh? I'm sure we have another lantern battery here somewhere."

But as Nigel looked, he noticed that the oxygen levels were dangerously low.

"Can we go home now, Mr. Strawberry?" asked Susie.

To everyone's delight Marianne's voice was on the radio. *"Nigel, we are right above you. We're lowering the cables now. Is everybody okay down there?"*

Nigel smiled. "Excellent, dearest! Well one little girl is rather pouty, and *somebody* needs a diaper change . . . I shan't say whom. . . ."

Nigel winked at the babies.

Suddenly a cable clamped onto the bathysphere from above.

"Here we go, children!"

Suddenly a huge jolt rocked the bathysphere.

Nigel looked up.

The babies screamed as they all stared straight into the eye of a giant squid!

The giant squid's long slippery tentacles snaked around the bathysphere. Its huge eye peered at them with interest.

The babies gasped, frightened.

But Tommy stepped toward the window, fascinated by the huge creature.

"Smashing!" Nigel exclaimed. "Why, it's the *Architeuthis*, commonly known as the giant squid! Isn't she magnificent?"

Tommy smiled, listening to Nigel talk. He didn't understand what had happened to Nigel Strawberry. Or why he had been acting so strange. But now Tommy knew that his hero was back to normal.

"If only I had a camera . . . ," Nigel said wistfully.

Susie looked at her camera. Then she thrust it into Nigel's hands. "Here, Mr. Strawberry!"

Delighted, Nigel held the camera up to the glass. He snapped a picture. "Sixty feet long and two tons of boneless flesh!"

The instant photo popped out of the camera, and Nigel eagerly looked at the picture. Then he sighed. It was all black, except for a small streak of light.

"Oh, your picture didn't come out," Susie said.

Nigel peered back out into the dark waters. The giant squid was gone.

"Well, that's probably as it should be,"

Nigel said. "You see, children, the giant squid has never been seen alive before. I suppose this marvel of nature will be our little secret. What do you say?"

The babies nodded and smiled.

• • •

Moments later the bathysphere bobbed to the surface. Spike and Eliza watched it as it approached the shore.

"See, Spike?" Eliza said. "You saved your babies—without your nose."

"Yeah, I guess I did," admitted Spike. "Thanks a heap, kiddo." Spike sniffed around. "Hey, I think the sniffer's coming back!"

Spike turned to Darwin and sniffed. "Hey, Chimpboy. I have two words for you: col-ogne.

Angelica was the first to step out of the bathysphere. She rushed into her parents' arms.

Then Chuckie, Kimi, Phil, and Lil appeared. Their parents nearly wept as they picked them up and hugged.

Susie came out carrying Dil. Didi took Dil and hugged Susie tight.

At last Nigel Thornberry came out carrying Tommy. "And who does *this* chap belong to?"

Tommy took Nigel's hand and led him to his father.

With tears in his eyes Stu picked up Tommy and hugged him tight. Then he offered his hand to Nigel. "Nice to meet you, Mr. Thornberry. And . . . thank you."

Tommy smiled. He had never dreamed that one day his favorite TV hero would get to meet his other favorite hero—his dad.

Then Marianne stepped forward to greet Nigel. "Honey, I'd like you to meet Stu Pickles," she said, choking up. "He made the coconut radio that . . . saved your lives."

"Ever so grateful, Mr. Pickles," said Nigel. Then Nigel looked over at Tommy. "I have a feeling I wouldn't be here without this little one, either." Nigel winked at Tommy.

"Oh, Nigel," Marianne said. "I was so worried."

"I confess, I was too," Nigel said. "I hated the thought of our last family meal being shortchanged because"—he choked back a sob—"because we had to go find a leopard."

Debbie was feeling kind of emotional herself, but she tried to hide it. "Aw, those muffins weren't that good anyway."

"Your father's right," Marianne admitted to her kids. "We lost sight of what's really important—spending time together." She wiped at the tears that threatened to fall.

Eliza and Debbie exchanged a glance.

"Oh, Mom," Eliza said.

"Come on, girls. Come on, Donnie." She pulled them all into a group hug. Donnie made a running leap onto Nigel's shoulders. Darwin, feeling a little left out, shoved his way in for a hug.

Sniffling, Nigel patted his pocket. "Hankie must be here somewhere. . . ."

"Oh, sorry, Dad," apologized Eliza. "It was my turn to do the laundry."

"No one's doing any laundry—or any work," said Marianne. "Starting right now we're on vacation!"

CHAPTER 19

At sunset the Pickles, Finsters, and DeVilles gathered for dinner. They were on the roof of the Commvee, and they were being pulled back to civilization by the SS *Lipschitz*.

They all gazed up at the cruise ship, where they had planned to be. The ship was all lit up with colorful lights. Music wafted on the breeze. The passengers were dancing and partying on deck.

Tommy and his friends were sitting around a lantern, drinking juice and eating cookies.

"Well, guys, we did it," Tommy said proudly. "We founded Nigel Strawberry, and no one's mad anymores!"

"Pickles," Angelica said, "you might grow up to be just like Nigel Strawberry after all."

Tommy beamed. "Thanks, Angelica. But I think I'll grow up to be just like my daddy."

"I propose a toast!" Didi announced. "To the best vacation we ever had!"

Everyone laughed and clinked glasses.

Tommy looked up at the starry night sky and smiled. Everything was back to normal again. He'd met Nigel Strawberry at last. And they'd had a marvelous adventure called a "vacation."

Not bad for a bunch of babies.

ABOUT THE AUTHOR

Cathy East Dubowski has written more than one hundred books for children, including The Wild Thornberrys *Gift of Gab* and *Hanging On to Home* (cowritten with husband Mark Dubowski). She lives in Chapel Hill, North Carolina, with Mark and their two daughters, Lauren and Megan. And while they don't have Eliza Thornberry's special talent, they do their best to talk to their pets Macdougal and Morgan (golden retrievers), Carster and Coconut (hamsters), Ramona (guinea pig), and Coco-Puffs (rabbit). Cathy writes on a computer in her office in an old red barn, which she shares with various insects, lizards, and the occasional field mouse.